Hook, Line, & Tinkerbell

HARMONY A. HAUN

ISBN: **978-1-961040-99-1** Paperback

ISBN: **978-1-961040-97-7** E-book

ISBN: **978-1-961040-98-4** Hardback

First edition

Author Contact: harmonyahaunauthor@gmail.com

IG: Harmonya.haun_author

Playlist

Each chapter has their own dedicated song linked to the top, but feel free to access the entire playlist (even more songs) by clicking this link to Spotify

Or by scanning the QR code below. Happy listening!

Preface & Triggers

This is a spin-off to Unforgivable Sins, my dark romance Peter Pan reimagining. Although this can be read first or as a standalone, I don't recommend it as it will give away the plot to Unforgivable Sins, should you decide to read it later. Also, it may prevent you from truly connecting with the characters and the storyline. So, if you haven't read Unforgivable Sins yet, go read it now, then come back!

As always, writing and reading is highly suggestive. Our individual lives and experiences cause us to have different perspectives and responses to certain things than anyone else. It is never my intention to write something inaccurate or hurtful, but please keep in mind, this is a work of fiction. Just because I write it, doesn't mean that's how I see the world.

Also, please protect yourself by reading the trigger warning below:

POTENTIAL TRIGGERS: Adult language and content, voyeurism, exhibitionism, death, killing, talk of rape/pedophilia (implied but not detailed), physical abuse by a partner, torture (implied but not detailed), mention of substance abuse, betrayal.

If you ever need to talk to someone, please seek help.
National Sexual Assault Line: 1-800-656-4673
Suicide & Crisis Line: 1-800-273-8255

Dedication

This book is dedicated to my readers!
To everyone who read Unforgivable Sins.
To everyone who requested Hook and Tink's story.

The fact that you asked for this makes it so incredibly special
to me, and I cannot thank you enough for your excitement and
support.
XOXO

Hook, Line, & Tinkerbell

Prologue

Purgatory is too often a misunderstood place. Contrary to popular belief, it's not actually controlled by the Angel of Death who oversees it. Oh, he's a crucial part no doubt. His ability to walk both the Earthly plane and Limbo brings him immense and deeply personal knowledge about the souls entering his domain. But that knowledge isn't his to freely give.

It's for these to discover.

Souls entering Limbo have unfinished business holding them back from moving on to Heaven or Hell, their Afterlife. This usually means the person was unwilling or unable to face their truths while alive, and in order for them to find peace, must confront those truths while in Purgatory. Peter Sinnclair, also known as Sinn, the Angel of Death, is only allowed to guide souls on this journey, he cannot force them. It doesn't happen often, but on occasion, some souls flat-out refuse to confront their darkest and truest selves.

They become lost souls.

Souls that remain in Purgatory for eternity, never to move on, never to find their peace. Thus, the realm has often been called, The Land of Never.

To some, this may not sound like such a bad end as surely it must be better than spending an eternity in Hell. But they'd be wrong, because even in Hell souls find their peace while souls in Purgatory continue to exist in an in-between state. They're still susceptible to death, only death of a different kind.

Their final death.

If a soul experiences final death in Purgatory, their body deteriorates or is fed to the mermaids, and the soul is lost to a world of complete darkness. Nothingness. Forever to exist alone with no light, no sound, no feeling other than emptiness. It is the worst kind of torture, and the worst possible end.

And then there are very special cases. Cases that exist outside the normal rules of Purgatory. These souls are the most difficult to help because even when they *do* face their truths, they remain stuck. They remain in Limbo, burdened with the knowledge of their harsh truths, and unable to pass into their Afterlife. Therefore, they're unable to find peace.

They are not in control.

They are not lost.

They are something else entirely.

Chapter 1

Misery by Kaleido

The Jolly Roger leaves port one soul too heavy. A soul I am *not* looking forward to hosting for…I don't know how long. Tink was forced onto this ship, she didn't choose it like I did. Granted, my choice was somewhat forced when I volunteered to follow Peter to Purgatory for his punishment. As his big brother, how could I not come with him to make sure he'd be ok?

I knew what I was signing up for when I took on the role of Captain of this ship. Tink, on the other hand, has no fucking clue. Not to mention her attitude is hard enough to take in small doses, now I have to deal with it constantly. I don't fucking need this shit and neither does my crew or the souls we ferry.

The souls heading to Heaven are easy enough. They may be a bit nervous, understandably, but they don't require much work. The souls headed to Hell…yeah, not so much. As one would expect, they need the small amount of light we offer them on their final journey, and Tink doesn't have a single ounce of light in her.

The only thing that made her even halfway tolerable before was the fact that she was madly loyal and dedicated to Peter. I won't say she was in love with him, though I'm sure she thinks she was, but she was definitely obsessed with him. Her jealousy led her to betray him when she tried to force Wendee to move on. He, in turn, banished her from his land. Now she has absolutely no reason to be anything other than her true self. Hateful and angry.

And she's on my fucking ship.

What the hell kind of bad karma did I tally up to deserve this shit? Sighing heavily, I focus on steering out of port and into open water. I'm not sure I'll stick to the six months at sea rule, only docking to load souls before heading back out. I may need to escape onto land every time we port just so I can get away from this mess.

Closing my eyes, I tilt my head back as we pick up speed, reveling in the feel of the wind on my face. It rushes through my beard and blows my hair back, cooling my neck. My long trench coat flaps in the breeze, and the sound of my crew yelling instructions to each other soothes me as we ready ourselves for yet another journey to The Gates.

"Looks like smooth sailing, Captain."

"Good. One less thing to worry about." Opening my eyes slowly, I drink in the horizon. The setting sun paints the sky in a new masterpiece every evening and I can't wait to see the beautiful show it has in store for us today. It's one of my favorite times to be on deck.

Sunset and sunrise.

A spot of vibrant green against the light pink pastels of the sky catches my attention. It would appear I'm not the only one attempting to enjoy the view. Tink leans on the rail, looking out toward the horizon too. I sigh again. I suppose it's my duty as Captain to welcome her on board and show her around.

"That one going to be a problem?" Smee quirks an eyebrow as his observant green eyes move from her to me.

All I can do is shake my head and shrug. "I hope not, but if I was a betting man—"

"You *are* a betting man." He chuckles.

"Well, I bet the answer is yes, Smee. She's going to be a fucking problem."

"Figured."

Just like the other crew members, Smee is a lost soul,

forever stuck in the Land of Never. Most lost souls are the ones who were headed to a fiery eternity, but instead of crossing The Gate, they chose to remain here. It doesn't happen as often as you'd think, but it happens. Needless to say, my crew isn't the *Saintliest* bunch. Surprisingly, Smee was headed to Heaven. He's my first mate, someone I trust implicitly, but even after all these years together, he's never confided in me. I don't know why he chose to stay instead of finding his peace in Heaven.

Finally meeting his gaze, I'm thankful I don't see judgment in his eyes. Not that I had a choice bringing her onto this ship. "Take the wheel and call if you need me."

"Yes, Sir," he says respectfully. Patting him on his shoulder, I take my leave. May as well get this over with.

My resolve slowly starts to fade as each stride across deck takes me closer and closer to what I'm certain is going to be my death. Well…ok, unlike the lost souls, I can't die here. But that doesn't mean she won't *try* to kill me, or hell, try to throw me overboard at least. The thought of her small body trying to lift me over the rail makes me chuckle. Stopping halfway, I take a swig of courage from my flask, the delicious burn of rum sliding down my throat fueling me forward.

Easing up alongside her, I mirror her casual pose and lean against the rail. The sky is now awash with color as bright oranges and reds paint the lower hanging clouds. The urge to spread my wings and launch off deck tingles down my spine. A sunset is beautiful from below the clouds but it's nothing compared to the view from above them.

"Do you want something? Or is interrupting my peace enough for you?" she asks, without ever taking her eyes off the sky.

I return the gesture. "Let's get one thing clear. You're on *my* ship, therefore, you're the one interrupting *my* peace."

"It wasn't my choice to be here," she snaps.

"Nor was it mine," I snap back. I'm not usually one to be

harsh or cruel. I've always been the light-hearted one, but this little she-devil tests my patience the second she opens her disrespectful mouth. Silence envelopes us for a few seconds before I push on, trying to embody my normal easy and positive tone. "Considering the alternatives, I think this was the best option."

She scoffs. "Speak for yourself."

I hold back a frustrated sigh. "Oh, so you would have rather been fed to Serene or had your soul ripped from your body?" I question, watching her closely. Her stubborn ass keeps her jaw clenched shut and eyes locked on the horizon, refusing to acknowledge me or the truth. "Yeah, that's what I thought."

Tugging at my beard, I keep my hands occupied to refrain from throwing *her* overboard. I desperately want to be anywhere else in the world than standing here with someone who despises everyone and everything for no damn reason but…here the fuck I am.

"Look, you're here and you're going to remain here for the foreseeable future, so you may as well get used to it," I say matter-of-factly.

"That's never going to happen."

"It is if you want to survive on this ship. The crew won't take kindly to you being here and not pulling your weight."

"Well, aren't you the all-powerful, all-commanding Captain? Make them like it," she says through clenched teeth.

She finally locks her angry hazel eyes with mine. I've never noticed how much green is mixed with her golden irises. Then again, I've only ever seen Tink a handful of times, all in the dim light of Sinful Delights, or under the cover of darkness when she asked me to meet her on the beach and tried to manipulate me into giving her gold dust.

Her arrogance despite the situation makes me chuckle. "I get it. You're used to having your way behind the bar, but this isn't Sinful

Delights, honey. You either get on board or prepare to be absolutely fucking miserable."

"That a threat?" Her angry eyes narrow, nostrils flaring.

I shake my head. "Not a threat. The truth. Fuck around and find out or get over yourself and your little pity-party and make a new home here, which is what I strongly suggest you do. Now…," I continue before she can argue some more, "let me show you around the ship and where you'll bunk."

My voice softens as I notice the bruising around her neck. The fact that she's standing here with only a few bruises is a testament to Peter's control. I know he wanted to kill her. And even though she may have earned his rage, the bruises are hard to look at.

Her lips press together firmly as she fights the urge to snap back with some feisty retort. Waving her arm out dramatically, she gestures for me to move. "Lead the way, *Captain*," she says sarcastically, with a cheesy, fake smile plastered on her face.

This fucking woman.

The crew eyes us warily as we pass by. They've all been briefed about the new, *reluctant* crew member. We're used to new souls coming on board constantly, but permanent newcomers are rare. I don't blame their unease or their curiosity. This bunch is a tight-knit group, and I can't say I'm not nervous about how all of this is going to unfold. I can't help my own curiosity at how Tink is going to respond and handle her new reality. Sinful Delights is known for its depravity, but it mostly leans toward violence due to the owner, a miserable Angel of Death. I am also curious if that will change now
that he has Wendee.

The Jolly Roger has its own depravity, though it's not known by anyone outside of this crew. What happens on this ship stays on this ship. Even the ruler of this domain is unaware of it, and I'd like to keep it that way. I'm not usually one for secrets between my brother and I, but there are just some things better left at sea. The only sense of relief I feel about having Tink here is knowing she's not welcome on land. There's no way my brother would ever be ok with seeing her again much less speaking with her, so our secrets will remain secrets.

The bulk of the ship is below deck. It's honestly more like a five-star hotel than a ship. We have a full kitchen and storage area, a laundry room, a lounge (where the new souls being transported are currently gathered), huge locker room style bathrooms equipped with stalls to shower, and one large jacuzzi tub.

"How the fuck is all of this down here?" she asks, wide-eyed.

I smirk. "It's a Divine ship, Tink, captained by an angel. What did you think it was going to be like? Rotting wood and moldy cells?"

Her eyes roll dramatically. "Obviously not this."

"The bedrooms are quite large and fit several people in each. The crew usually like to bunk together instead of separately. They're like a litter of puppies, just dogpiling onto each other."

She scoffs. "Well, I am definitely *not* doing that."

"That's your prerogative. Boring but...." Shrugging my shoulders, I turn my attention away from her and push open the door to a smaller room. "You can stay here. It's the smallest room, but since you don't plan on sharing it, it should suit your needs just fine."

She walks inside and looks around. Her bags have already been placed on the bed. "I'm the door at the end of the hall should you need anything. You can sulk and keep to yourself tonight, but tomorrow you're a part of this crew whether you like it or not. I'm assigning Smee to be your mentor. He'll teach you everything you need to know about crewing. I know you're used to being solo behind the bar, but we do things as a team here. Like I said, the sooner you can get on board with that the better it will be for all of us."

Standing in the middle of the room with her arms crossed, she gives me a death glare. Yeah, this is definitely going to be interesting.

"Do you need anything before I leave you alone for the night?"

"I don't *need* anything from you."

Shaking my head, I sigh in defeat. "Then I'll leave you to it." Before closing the door, I make one last request. "Tink…fair warning, stay in your room tonight."

"Why?"

"Just…stay in your damn room."

"What? Am I your prisoner now?" she asks, her hands moving to her hips.

"No…," I say slowly and clearly, "just until you get a bit more…settled, I'm encouraging you stay put. Wander at your own risk."

"What the fuck does that me—"

"Goodnight." Cutting her off, I close the door behind me. Walking back down the hall, I jog up the steps to the top deck, needing the open air desperately.

Taking a deep breath of salty sea air, I slide both hands through my hair knowing damn well Tink won't listen to my suggestion just to spite me. Yeah…this is most definitely going to be interesting.

Chapter 2

Throwing myself down on the bed, I sigh heavily. I can't believe this is happening. Just yesterday, I was on cloud nine knowing Wendee was headed to Hell and I was about to have Sinn all to myself again. Not that I ever *had* him, but life was at least about to go back to normal when everything fucking changed. Everything twisted. My world was flipped upside down and the ground was literally ripped from beneath my feet.

I can never step foot on land again.

After spending a hundred and fifty years with Sinn, his banishment hurts more than anything else he could have done to me. That's what Hook doesn't get. I *wish* he had fed me to Serene or pulled the soul from my body. Either of those two options would be better than *this*. Stuck on this fucking ship, with Mr. Fucking Sunshine, while the man I love is with another woman and not thinking twice about me.

A hundred and fifty years tossed to the sea like it meant nothing to him. Like *I* meant nothing to him. After all of the years I was a constant and loyal companion, cleaning up his messes, and standing by his side when no one else dared. Well, no one except Hook, but I don't think Hook has ever understood Sinn. Not really. Not like me. And this is what I get for all those years of loyalty? I scoff and push myself off the bed, needing to move. The last thing I need is to be left alone with my thoughts right now. Nothing good has ever come with me being alone with my mind and yet, that's how I've spent most of my life.

Alone.

At least that's what my life has been like since I died and came to Purgatory. I don't remember my life before waking up here. Not one second or sliver of a memory remains. Sinn says it's because whatever I suffered on Earth was *"traumatizing"* and I don't want to face it, yet he won't tell me what happened even though he knows. Fucking self-discovery and all that bullshit.

I could always do what I did to Wendee to make her remember. I could take gold dust. But honestly, I've never had the desire to know what happened to me. What does it matter anyway? That life is in the past, and my Afterlife is long gone too. I don't need the knowledge of whatever trauma I experienced. Being on this prison of a ship is going to be trauma enough.

Hook wasn't kidding when he said the room was small. There's only a queen-size bed and one dresser which doesn't leave room for much else. There's definitely no room for dogpiling, thank fuck. A small round window allows the fading sunlight to filter in, but it's too high up for me to see out of. A door next to the bed opens up to a small closet. It's not much but again, Hook is right, it will fit my needs just fine because I don't have much. Though I do wish I had a private bathroom. This community-style living and sharing spaces shit is *not* my jam.

It's not that I want to get settled on this ship, but I know I don't have a choice, so I keep myself busy by unpacking my bags. As far as becoming a part of this crew goes, that's a different story. I don't plan on doing anything to fit in. If they want to shun me for it, all the better. I'm just fine being on my own.

Unfortunately, unpacking doesn't take long, and I'm once again sprawled across the bed. My damn treacherous mind keeps going back to Sinn and how incredibly angry he was when he found out what I'd done. Gently touching my sore throat, I remember his hand there in a crushing grip and of looking in a mirror, the marks of his anger blossoming in purple and green around my neck. I seriously thought he was going to kill me. And I wish he had, so I wouldn't be lying here clinging to that awful memory just to remember what it felt like for him to touch me.

Sighing, I throw my arm back down on the bed. What the fuck is wrong with me? Why the hell am I still thinking about a man who never wanted anything to do with me? Am I that fucking depraved? Am I that fucking lonely?

"Don't answer that," I mutter to myself.

And then there's the way Hook looked at me when he saw the bruises. Just fucking great. He's always been decent to me, at least I have that. He's always looked at me like…well, not like we're friends, but also not like I'm garbage either. He's always seen me in a way Sinn never did. Hook sees me as a *person*, someone who still has a soul, and I don't want that to change. But the last thing I want is his pity.

The sound of my stomach growling gives me something else to focus on. Food. I haven't eaten all day, but the idea of food does nothing for me. Despite my stomach protesting, I have no appetite, but that doesn't mean I have no interest in nosing around the kitchen. I don't give two shits about Hook's *suggestion* to stay in my room tonight. If this is my new home, I'll be damned if I'm confined to this small room.

Pushing off the bed, I quickly walk to the door and throw it open, marching back down the hall with an attitude that dares anyone to try and fucking stop me. In fact, I wish a motherfucker would. It would give me a reason to let out all my frustration and anger. To my disappointment, no one does.

Strolling into the empty kitchen, I start opening every cabinet and drawer, taking stock of what's available, which is *everything*.

This is the fanciest kitchen I've ever seen. Granted, I only remember the one in Sinn's building, which was phenomenal, but this one is even more impressive. There's every appliance imaginable, from regular toasters and coffee pots to toaster ovens and commercial grade barista machines. Not to mention the oversized stainless-steel appliances, gleaming like gems, and a refrigerator stocked top to bottom with groceries. There's everything from healthy stuff like fresh fruit and vegetables, yogurt, and juices, to sodas, cookie dough, and a shit ton of ice cream. The pantry is packed with more of the same, a mix of healthy and delicious. I may not have an appetite for food, but junk food is a different story. Greedily taking a pack of Double Stuf Oreos, I tear into it, stuffing a whole one in my mouth.

"Mm." Closing my eyes, I savor the delicious mix of crunchy chocolate and smooth cream.

My eyes snap open and I stop chewing, listening intently. My moan just echoed like crazy. Wait…there it is again. Not my moan, but someone else's. Clutching the Oreos to my chest, I quietly walk back down the hall, toward the sound.

More odd sounds and voices join the first as I get closer to the lounge Hook pointed out earlier. Leaning against the wall, I inch myself to the open doorway and peek inside as inconspicuously as possible. I have to slam my hand down on my mouth to stifle the coughing fit from gasping and swallowing a mouthful of Oreo down the wrong pipe. Plastering myself to the wall and out of sight, I clear my throat and slowly get control of my breathing.

The heartbeat pounding against my other hand tells me I'm definitely awake and not dreaming.

Holy shit.

Squeezing my eyes shut, I try to think rationally because there's no way I saw what I think I did. *Did I?* No. No way. There's no damn way. *Is there?* The repeated and uncertain thoughts make me feel crazy, and there's only one way to be certain. Taking a deep breath, steadying my nerves, I look through the doorway again.

Holy shit.

It takes my mind a few seconds to figure out exactly what I'm seeing, but once it does, I'm frozen in shock. There are naked bodies everywhere. I don't know where to look, and every time my eyes land on something, it's too insane and I look somewhere else. Except, nowhere is safe.

An orgy.

Holy shit, I'm looking at an orgy. Men and women clutter every open space, up against walls, on the floor, limbs tangled with limbs. My eyes finally land on a table off to the side where a woman is sprawled on top of it. A man stands between her legs, fucking her, while two others stand at each side getting hand jobs and touching her body, while another woman straddles her face, getting her own pleasure while she kisses one of the men.

All at once the sounds come crashing down around me. I'm inundated by moans of pleasure and flesh slapping against flesh, voices screaming, some begging and some commanding. It's absolute and utter madness. I have no idea who's a part of the crew and who are the souls being transported, but they all look like they are thoroughly enjoying themselves.

My eyes go back to the man fucking the woman on the table. His sun-kissed body is on full display, and I can't help but appreciate what I see. He's tall, though not as tall as Hook or Sinn. Then again, no one else here is an angel and the angelic brothers are in a league of their own. Still, this man is definitely holding his own. His muscular body pounds into the woman with ruthlessness, his large hands holding her in place as he thrusts into her in long, hard strokes. His firm ass looks good from this angle, and his legs are strong and steady. I can't quite see his dick, but from the way he's thrusting, it must be just as impressive as the rest of him.

He must sense my eyes on him because he looks up and to the side, sending a lock of blonde hair falling over his forehead, slightly blocking his vision. But those green eyes still manage to lock on to me. He never hesitates or stops fucking the woman. He just smirks and winks.

Gasping, I jump back into the hallway, hiding myself once again. Before I can process what just happened, I practically run back down the hall, past the kitchen, and crash into my room. Slamming the door behind me, I lean into it, still clutching Oreos to my chest. My knees finally give out and I slide to the floor, trying to catch my breath.

"What in the fuck was that?" Since I'm by myself, I'm not expecting an answer, but I would really fucking like one. Hook's warning echoes in my mind.

Just until you get a bit more…settled, I'm encouraging you stay put. Wander at your own risk.

Is that what he was trying to keep me from seeing? I mean, fucking obviously. Right? An orgy is not normal and it's something I certainly never expected to see *here*. I've seen my fair share of sexual acts at Sinful Delights, and I'm no virgin, but I've never seen anything like what I just saw.

Does he know what goes on here? He's the captain, he must know. I didn't see him in the mix of bodies though, and I would have *definitely* noticed him if he had been there. Does he just allow this to happen on his ship? Does he participate? He was always flirty when he visited Sinful Delights. Hell, I saw him leave with women on several occasions. *But this!* This is on a whole new level, and I don't know how to process what I just saw.

Or how I responded.

I'm shook. Obviously, I'm traumatized, as I've been reduced to a confused mess sitting on the floor, barely breathing. For the millionth time in the past twenty-four hours, I find myself thinking, *I can't believe this is happening.*

Once the shock starts wearing off, I feel repulsion taking its place. I am *not* ok with this. This is where I have to live for the foreseeable future, and I refuse to be locked up in this damn room every night. This is not normal. I'll have a talk with Hook about this first thing in the morning.

Feeling more like myself, resolved with my decision, I push off the floor and throw myself down on the bed again. Only, when I close my eyes, all I can see are green eyes winking at me and sweaty bodies everywhere. I shove another Oreo into my mouth and try desperately to think of something else. Anything else.

Finally managing to tear my mind free from tonight, I settle on my comfort zone. Sinn. Though the only images flashing across my mind are the ones where he's with Wendee. I give up on the Oreos and on getting any sleep. Curling onto my side, I stare into the growing darkness, trying to calm my racing thoughts. The sound of the waves crashing against the ship only adds to my restlessness.

I would rather be in Hell than on this ship right now. I don't know how I'm going to survive this. I may just throw myself overboard and let Serene have her way with me.

Chapter 3

Beep.

    Beep.

        Beep.

The sound of steady beeping echoes in my mind, seeming faint and distant, but it's quickly replaced by knocking that pulls me from sleep. My surroundings are barely visible in the dim glow of dawn filtering through the window above me. After a few seconds, I remember where I am and pull the covers over my head with a groan. I don't remember falling asleep, but if the way I feel is any indication, it definitely wasn't long enough.

The knocking turns into banging, followed by a deep male voice that isn't Hook's. "I'm giving you thirty more seconds before I come in and *make* you get up. I hope you're decent."

Shit. Did I lock the door last night? It doesn't matter. He can bang and yell and come in to try and get me up, but I don't plan on leaving this bed for at least another few hours. Hell, I may just stay in bed all day. It's a better alternative to anything else happening on this ship.

The door opens and someone steps inside. I'm huddled under the covers, so I don't know who it is, and I don't care.

"Come on, it's time to get up. There's a lot to learn."

"Go away," I mumble.

"Not gonna happen, princess. This isn't a free ride or a

vacation."

"No, it's Hell."

"We can do this the easy way or the hard way. You choose."

The covers are forcefully pulled off me, and the cool morning air sends goosebumps racing across my skin. I'd probably shiver if I wasn't so pissed.

I bolt upright. "What the fuck! You have no right to—" The words get stuck in my throat as I finally lay eyes on my tormentor. The image of him fucking that lady while winking at me floods my memory, causing my body to flush with heat and welcome the cool morning air.

His green eyes are dark and hard to see in the dim light, but they somehow still manage to sparkle with amusement. "Oh, I assure you, I have every right to do whatever is necessary to get you out of this bed and up on deck."

So, this must be Smee. Hook said he'd assign him to teach me everything I need to know about being on this ship. Of course, it would be him that caught me watching last night. Just my luck. Pushing the image of his very golden, very muscular, and very naked body out of my head, I hold on to my anger and climb out of bed, thankful that I'm still fully dressed in yesterday's clothes.

"There, see. That wasn't so hard now, was it?" he asks mockingly.

Stepping up to him, I grab ahold of the covers and yank them out of his grip. He doesn't fight me. Instead, he just stands there, looking down at me with that same smirk from last night and laughter in his eyes. I hate that he appears to be laughing at me without actually laughing at me.

Narrowing my eyes, I let my anger control my words as I look up at him defiantly. "I would tell you to go suck a dick, but I think you'd actually like it."

"What's wrong with sucking a dick?" he counters. "Maybe you

should try it. I bet some good dick would help ease some of this frustration I'm sensing. Hell…," he shrugs, "I'm willing to test the theory if you are."

Hugging the covers tight to my body, I scoff in disgust. "In your dreams, pal. Now get the fuck out of my room," I order as I throw myself back down on the bed, pulling the covers over my head.

"The hard way then."

The sound of footsteps retreating makes me smile. *Well, that was easier than I thought.* I sigh and close my eyes, curling into myself and attempting to go back to sleep. I'm almost there when the sound of footsteps echo in the room again.

"I told you to leave me—"

A loud gasp escapes my throat as ice-cold water soaks through the covers and into me. I didn't shiver with the cool air before, but I sure as hell do now. Fighting with the heavy, drenched blanket, I finally manage to get it off me but all I can do is sit in the middle of the bed, shaking uncontrollably, hair plastered to my face and my clothes suctioned to my skin.

"I did warn you," an unexpected voice says smugly. "Now get up, get your shoes on, and let's go."

It's Hook. Smee must have gone running to daddy to tattle on me like a little snitch. I'm definitely having words with him later, but right now, I really want to give Hook a piece of my mind. Only my teeth are chattering too violently to speak.

"If I have to drag you out of that bed Tink, it's not going to be pretty."

"You…wouldn't…dare," I manage to stutter.

Hook smiles. But it's not his usual, sexy *'hey, how are you doing'* smile that I've seen him use on women several times. No, it's a devious *'oh, this is going to be fun'* smile. And before I know it, his hands are on me, pulling me across the bed. Then, my world is flipped upside down as I'm lifted and thrown over his shoulder. Adrenaline and anger course through my veins, overpowering the numbing cold in my bones, and I'm finally able to move.

"Put me down!" I scream, attempting to kick my legs, but it's no use. Hook has them secured in his strong arms. So, I resort to pounding my fists into his back but it's like hitting a brick wall.

"Calm your ass down." A loud, wet smack causes me to gasp again, the air getting lodged in my chest for a few seconds. I'm more shocked than pissed.

"Did you just *spank* me?" I ask, appalled.

"It got you to stop fighting, didn't it?" His deep voice rumbles through his chest as he starts climbing the steps that lead to the deck.

I'm about to start yelling and cussing again when the chill of the open-air bites against my wet skin making me gasp yet again. I'm not sure what's worse, the sting on my bare skin or the jeans and tank top practically freezing against my body.

Hook attempts to set me down on my feet but my body convulses from the cold and my legs give out, sending me sprawling on my ass. He could have caught me, but he didn't. Asshole.

"Next time, get up when Smee tells you to. Follow direction and this won't happen."

"It's fucking...freezing...out here," I say through ragged breaths.

"You should have thought about that before being a little brat."

"I'm not staying...up here...like this," I struggle to say. "I'll...freeze...to death."

"Again, you should have that about that. Actions always have consequences, Tink. These are your consequences. I warned you yesterday and Smee warned you today. This is going to be as easy or as hard as you make it, but you're the one in control of how it goes."

"Ok, ok," I concede. "Can I...at least...go change?"

"No," he commands, with no room for argument.

"But—" I try anyway.

"It'll warm up soon enough. Start moving your body and get to work, that will help."

Hook motions to someone behind me and a few moments later Smee is standing next to him. Smee is quite large. It was evident last night when his impressive body was on full display, but he looks small standing next to Hook. Jesus, I guess I never really noticed just how overwhelming Hook's presence is. Before, I'd always seen him relaxed and laughing, flirting like his life depended on it. It probably didn't help that my attention was always on Sinn.

Now, he stands before me portraying every bit of the commanding captain that he is. There's not one trace of playfulness in his eyes or body language. His tone is cold and direct as he addresses Smee.

"Keep me posted on her attitude and work ethic."

"Yes, Sir," Smee says.

Hook glances down at me but doesn't say anything else before storming off to do whatever the hell it is that he does. Then, Smee's eyes are on me, and that stupid smirk pulls at his lips.

"I did warn you," he says, only slightly self-satisfied.

"Bite me." I'm exhausted and worn down, so the words don't come out as harsh as I'd like.

Leaning down, he offers his hand. Reluctantly, I take it, letting him pull me to my feet. He keeps ahold of my hand and leans down further, whispering in my ear.

"I think you'd like being bitten."

Pulling my hand out of his, I stagger backward, trying to get my stiff legs to work properly. It doesn't help that the rock of the ship feels like an earthquake, throwing off my balance. "Maybe you shouldn't think at all. That small brain of yours is going to constantly get you into trouble."

He shrugs. "Small brain, big dick. I like my odds for trouble."

I scoff. "You're disgusting."

"You didn't seem all that disgusted last night as you watched me fuck. In fact, it seemed like you rather enjoyed the show."

My cheeks heat as blood rushes to my face. As much as I want to be upset about blushing in front of him, again, the heat feels too good to be mad at it. But my blush has nothing to do with Smee personally. He's attractive enough but he doesn't get my pulse pumping. My body reacted to what I saw, but my body din't want *him*.

"I didn't," I assure him, rolling my eyes. Before he can continue down this ridiculous conversational path, I change the subject. "So, what the fuck am I supposed to learn up here?"

He's doing that thing, where he laughs at me without laughing at me, but I ignore him and look around. There are a handful of crew members on deck, all looking very at ease and not at all like the deck they're walking on is moving beneath their feet. As soon as I move to take a step, the ship jerks harder, causing me to lose my balance completely. Two strong arms reach out and steady me.

"Goddamn this ship," I say frustratedly, trying to right myself.

"You'll get used to it," Smee laughs softly.

"I don't *want* to get used to it. I don't even want to be here."

"I get it, but you are here, princess. The sooner you accept that, the better it will be for everyone."

"Ok, Hook Jr."

"You know we're both right, just stop being stubborn."

"I am not being—"

"Right." He cuts me off. "Some things you'll need to know about the ship. It's important that you understand some of the lingo. Prow or bow is what the front of the ship is called." He points in the direction we're moving, as if I couldn't figure out which part of the ship is the front on my own. "We typically say bow but either can come up. The back of the ship is the stern or aft." He points again and I roll my eyes. "We usually say stern. If you're looking toward the bow...," he faces forward, "starboard indicates the right side of the ship and port indicates the left. Any questions so far?"

"No. It's not exactly rocket science."

"Along the bottom of the railing you'll see slots. Those are scuppers which allow water that gets on deck to drain back into the sea. You'll also see them throughout the lower level as well."

He starts walking further onto the deck, toward the middle of the ship, and I stumble along behind him. My gaze follows where he points up. "This is the mainmast and way up there is the crow's nest. That's where we can get a look in every direction and try to avoid any storms or get an idea of how close we are to land."

"Are there a lot of storms out here?" I ask nervously.

I never really thought about life at sea, but the mention of storms reminds me that what Smee said is true. This isn't a vacation. This is my new reality and all the unknowns about how to survive this life are suddenly slamming into me.

He shrugs. "There used to be but we're pretty confident it will mostly be smooth sailing going forward."

"Why do you think that?"

"Because the land is tied to the Angel of Death and his emotions directly affect what happens out here on the water. And, well, since he's found his soulmate, we don't think the sea will be too angry anymore."

"Oh."

The mention of Sinn and Wendee instantly twists my insides. I've been in Purgatory a long time, but I never realized the world around me reacted to him. Then again, I never spent much time outside of Sinful Delights. Fuck, I've been so laser focused on Sinn that I never gave a shit about anything else. Myself included.

"You ok, princess? You look like you're going to hurl."

"Fine," I grumble.

"It happens." He shrugs again. His demeanor is so nonchalant and laid back, which is the exact opposite of how I feel and that irks me even more. "The motion sickness, I mean. That'll get easier too."

"Right." I don't attempt to tell him my stomach is upset because of a man. Let him think whatever the fuck he wants.

"So, all of this...," he motions to the mess of ropes, chains, and sails, "is the ship's rigging. It looks like madness, but I promise there's a method to it all."

He starts walking again and I follow, though my path is more of a zigzag behind him. The sun is finally rising above the horizon, and I eagerly welcome the heat it's about to provide. My body is so cold it actually hurts.

We stop a few feet away from a set of steps that lead up to a small platform where Hook stands at the wheel. His long trench coat hides his body almost to his ankles, but I can tell how at ease he is up there, guiding his ship. His stance is strong and powerful. His feet are firmly grounded, and his broad shoulders are steady, keeping his grip light but firm around two spokes of the wheel as it gently moves from side to side. The sunlight illuminates his chestnut hair as it blows in the breeze, highlighting streaks of honey running through it.

"Enjoying the view, princess?" Smee's voice shakes me out of my daze.

Again, my cheeks heat and I'm pissed that he caught me staring. Not that I was staring *at* Hook. "I was just admiring how comfortable he is up there, that's all," I explain, pulling my eyes away from Hook and meeting Smee's. I roll my eyes at the look he's giving me but don't try to deny it further. Guilty people get nervous and try to deny accusations, but I have nothing to feel guilty about.

"Once we're sailing, it doesn't require much work to keep the ship on course, but we like to keep someone at the wheel most of the time anyway just in case we need to move quickly. It's usually me or Hook you'll see up there, very rarely anyone else."

"How long have you sailed with Hook?"

"Long enough to be his first mate."

"Fine, don't tell me. I don't actually give a shit anyway."

He chuckles. "So feisty."

"Are you going to introduce me to the rest of the crew?"

"You'll meet them at dinner tonight. We'll be docking at The Gates, so everyone will be free to sit down once the souls have all disembarked and been taken care of. Then, we head back to the Land of Never for another transport and do it all over again. Day after day."

"We'll be at The Gates already?"

He nods. "Yup. The journey isn't that long, just repetitive."

"How do you not get tired of the same shit every day?"

"There are new souls on board every few days. The routines may be the same, but every journey is different. We get to meet and talk with different people. We get to hear their stories, learn about what happened to them if they want to share, and if they don't...well, you saw how else we pass the time. And now, you're here." He bites his lip, his green eyes slowly skimming down my body before coming back up to meet mine. Jesus. I've never had someone be so blatantly in my face about sex before and my body

heats from the look in his eyes. "Trust me, there's nothing to get tired of."

"Says a *man*, who can get pleasure by sticking his dick into literally any hole, and you clearly never seem tired of finding one."

"Your aversion to sex has me thinking you've never really experienced great, mind-blowing sex."

I've had plenty of sex since I've been in Purgatory, but he's right, none of it has been great. Maybe I had great sex when I was alive, but I can't remember, so I honestly don't understand the hype. What's so good about it that someone craves it or wants it all the time? If I had great sex, would that make me change my mind? What even constitutes great sex? And mind-blowing sex? That just sounds like a hoax to me, but that doesn't mean I'm going to tell him he's right.

"And what did we say about you *thinking*?" I deflect. "You're not the brightest crayon in the box."

He laughs again. "You're going to be a lot of fun to have around, princess. Now, come on. Let's get you situated."

"Situated for what?"

"Your job for the day. Hook already told you; this isn't a free ride."

"And what exactly will be my job for the day?" I ask, crossing my arms over my stomach.

"Keeping the wood of the deck preserved and swelled is probably one of the most important things on this ship. We need it smooth, but not with mold or algae. We scrub it down with salt water, which is called swabbing, and you, princess, are going to take up the role of a swabbie until you're more familiar with everything on the ship." He smiles broadly, his green eyes laughing. "So, swabbie, you'll be washing the deck."

"Ugh," I groan. "You've got to be fucking kidding me."

Chapter 4

Dissolve by Softspoken

Wiping my dripping brow with the back of my arm, I curse the sun under my breath. It sits high in the sky, a blazing ball of fucking fire that feels like it's directed solely at me. There's not one cloud in the sky to save me. The gentle breeze from the movement of the ship does absolutely nothing to cool my overheated body, and I wish I was out of these damn jeans. I went from freezing my ass off to sweating my ass off. How can the weather in a single day be so drastically different?

"Fuck this," I say to myself as I lean the handle of the push broom against the rail.

Rolling my head from side to side, I lift my arms overhead and stretch, feeling my muscles pull tight. My back aches from being bent over, scrubbing at the deck, and my arms are practically Jell-O. I'm not used to physical labor like this, and I've been at it for hours. Funny how something becomes bigger than it appears when you start scrubbing every inch of it. I still have about one-third of the deck to finish but I'm already exhausted.

The loud and almost painful growl of my stomach solidifies my decision to take a break. All I had to eat yesterday were a few Oreos, and I don't know if it's because I haven't eaten or the physical exertion, but unlike yesterday, I'm starving. A glance up at the wheel shows me Smee is otherwise occupied. My eyes dart around but I don't see any sign of Hook. I take my chance and walk as quickly as possible across the deck, trying not to bring any more attention to myself than I already have with my stumbling.

First things first, I need to change out of these damn jeans. Heading to my room, I make it down the hallway unseen, slip inside and quickly close the door behind me, locking it this time. Tugging the jeans down my legs, I hop over to the dresser, tossing them aside. Opening a drawer, I pull out a pair of white shorts and shimmy into them. They're tight and barely cover my cheeks, but as hot as it is up on deck, I don't care who looks at my ass. Hell, if it gets any hotter, I may just say to hell with clothes period.

Pulling out a neon green sports bra that matches my hair, I exchange that for the sweaty tank top. Already feeling a million times cooler, I head back out toward the kitchen. My bare feet allow me to pad down the hallway silently. A huge grin splits my face as I walk into an empty kitchen. This is too easy.

Sauntering over to the huge fridge, I pull it open, scanning the shelves for something I can stuff my face with. A tin baking pan with foil covering the top catches my eye. I pull the foil back to reveal leftovers of a casserole of some sort.

"That'll work," I say cheerily to myself as I slide it off the shelf.

It takes a few seconds to find a plate and silverware, but once I do, I heave a huge portion of the casserole onto the plate, cover it with a paper towel, and toss it in the microwave. I return the casserole pan to the fridge and then proceed to the freezer, opening it up to find exactly what I'm looking for.

Ice.

Grabbing a chunk out of the bag, I lean back against the counter, waiting for my food to warm up, and start rubbing the ice on my heated skin. Leaning my head forward, I run the ice up and down the back of my neck before sliding it in front and across my chest. I close my eyes and let out a quiet moan at how good it feels.

"This doesn't look like washing the deck."

My eyes shoot open, and I jump, the ice falling down my bra and settling, melting rapidly between my breasts.

"Jesus Christ, Hook, you scared the shit out of me." He leans against the doorway, arms and ankles crossed as if content to just post up there forever. "How long have you been standing there?"

The microwave beeps loudly and I jump again, my hand slamming down on my chest. "Jesus!"

Hook laughs and pushes off the doorframe, striding into the kitchen like he owns the damn place. Then again, I guess he does. My eyes travel the large expanse of his body, now on display since his trench coat has been removed. I drink him in from his wind-blown hair, across his broad shoulders and muscular arms that are straining against the long sleeves of his white button-up shirt, down to where the black and white vest showcases his fit waist. But what really gets my heart rate up are the black leather pants that hug his muscular legs like a second skin before disappearing into black combat-style boots.

"Relax, Tink. It's ok that you're taking a break," he says, ignoring the fact that I just eye-fucked him as he walks to the microwave to remove my food, giving me a front row view of his incredibly sculpted ass.

He continues to give me his back as he walks to the island and places my plate down in front of a barstool. His vest is laced up in the back and actually looks more like a corset.

I look him over one more time before schooling my face the best I can. "Are you wearing a corset?" I ask blandly.

"Sit down and eat," he orders, completely ignoring my question. But his light tone tells me it's more like a peace offering than a harsh command.

"I can take a break *and* eat. What a relief. There for a minute I thought I was just going to be your slave," I say sarcastically, pulling myself up onto a black leather seat that looks more like a cozy chair than a barstool. It has a back and armrests that allow you to get comfortable and sit back instead of having to lean onto the island and get a kink in your spine.

He shakes his head. "There are no slaves on this ship. In fact, that's not even funny."

"I didn't mean it li—"

"I'm not sure how many times I have to tell you, this is going to be as easy or as hard as you want to make it. No one is going to stop you, or question you, or harass you, but you do need to pull your weight. Just do that and the crew won't have any issues with you."

"And you?" I ask defiantly.

"I don't want to have any issues with you either. We may have started off on the wrong foot, but regardless of what you think, this morning wasn't fun for me. But as the captain, I can't let you get away with anything I wouldn't let any other member of my crew get away with. If you don't want a repeat of this morning, then don't force my hand."

I can't help but roll my eyes like a scolded child. "I get it. I don't like it, I don't like *any* of this, but I get it," I concede as I finally lift the fork to my mouth.

Delicious flavors explode across my tongue, and I'm immediately consumed by it. I close my eyes and mumble, "Oh my god," before devouring another bite that elicits a moan.

"Actually, just Hook, but I'll take the compliment."

"You're joking, right?" I deadpan. "*You* made this?" I point to the pile of food on my plate with my fork as I stare dumbfounded at a ridiculously smug Hook.

"Why is that so hard to believe?"

"Because it's…." I look down at the food as if it will somehow give me the words I'm looking for. "It's…."

"Divine?" Hook offers up, the smirk on his lips widening to a cheesy grin that lights up his entire face. Staring into his sparkling cerulean eyes this close takes my breath away. His grin never falters as the silence stretches between us and I realize I'm staring.

Breaking our eye contact, I look down to scoop another bite of food onto my fork before replying. "Calm down there, wingboy, I wouldn't go *that* far. What kind of casserole is it?" I ask, before shoveling in another bite.

"It's a chicken and mushroom white lasagna, and you're eating it a day old. Tell me it's not divine after you've had it fresh."

I shake my head, ignoring his arrogance. "You really made this?"

He nods. "Cooking became a hobby. There's not much else to do onboard and it keeps me occupied. Oddly, I find cooking and baking to be rather soothing. I never had the desire before, but it's something I'm glad I discovered."

"Well, I wouldn't quit your day job or anything, but it is really good," I lie, taking another bite and holding back the urge to moan again. I will not give him this. I will not add to the cocky grin on his face.

He crosses his arms over his chest, his muscles straining against the shirt, and I notice color underneath the material. It's faint, but it's there. Is wingboy fucking tatted? All this time I thought he was the goody-two-shoes brother.

The angel who could do no wrong.

The angel who followed all of the rules.

And now I'm here, on his ship, where orgies are taking place and the captain wears tight leather pants, silver jewelry, and corsets, *and* he has tattoos? Color me fucking shocked...and incredibly intrigued. I lick my lips, only it's not the food I'm focused on anymore.

I realize I'm staring, again, and snap my eyes back up to Hook's to see if I've been caught, only to find his eyes lingering on my now wet and slightly parted lips.

I clear my throat and slide off the stool, grabbing my almost empty plate and heading to the sink. Taking a look around, I finally ask, "Where's the trash?"

Hook slowly closes the distance between us. I have to crane my neck back in order to keep looking at him which, at this point, I don't know if it's even a good idea, but I can't seem to help it. Something about him is magnetic, pulling me in.

"That's no way to treat my divine casserole. It doesn't deserve to be thrown in the trash. It deserves to be savored. Every. Last. Bite." He reaches out, taking the last piece between his fingers, holding it up for me to take. "Open," he demands softly.

And Lord help me, I do. I open my mouth and let him feed me the last bite, this one even more delicious than the first. My lips brush against his fingers and his thumb drags slowly across my bottom lip before he lifts it to his mouth. He slips his thumb between his lips and sucks it clean before doing the same to his pointer finger.

And I can't stop fucking staring.

"Finger-licking good," he says, barely above a whisper. And I barely keep from choking on the damn food I forgot to chew.

He smirks again before turning around and strolling back out of the kitchen, giving me another great view of his leather clad ass. Before he's out the door, he yells back, "Break is over! Finish washing the deck, swabbie!"

I narrow my eyes at him and growl my frustration, but he's oblivious to it. What in the hell just happened? I've seen Hook charm women left and right at Sinful Delights. I've always thought it was pathetic how easily they seemed to melt under his charm, but now that I've been on the receiving end of it, I'm no better.

My skin is burning up again, only this time it has nothing to do with the sun and everything to do with a devious and incredibly sexy captain. Did that really just happen? Did Hook just hand feed me?

And did I let him?

How have I never noticed him before?

Because there is *a lot* to notice. Those hints of color on his skin, barely noticeable beneath his shirt, have me itching to find out what exactly he's hiding. And yet, another part of me wants no part of any of this.

Shaking my head, I turn back to the sink and turn on the faucet, thoroughly scolding myself as I wait for the water to warm up. This is not where I want to be. This is not who I want to be with. None of this is what I chose. None of this is what I want. I can't lose sight of the fact that this is my punishment, not my happily ever after. For fuck's sake, I love Sinn.

Don't I?

I mean, at least, I did. Before everything happened with Wendee, I knew what I wanted, and this isn't it. Hook isn't it.

I angrily scrub my plate clean, but my thoughts are stuck on what happened moments ago. The feel of his thumb on my lip still lingers, so I angrily scrub at my lips too, trying to dispel the sensation and failing.

I yell my frustration to the ceiling and slam the plate into the drying rack.

"Still testy, I see. Apparently being hangry wasn't the cause of your anger."

I spin around and glare at Smee. He's laughing at me again, so I flip him off as I storm past him and seethe, "Bite me."

"Just give me the chance, princess. I think we could quell all that anger," he yells after me.

I don't dignify that with a response as I make my way back up to top deck. Hook is now standing at the wheel, his incredible frame taunting me and competing with the sun on who can make me hotter. Clenching my jaw, I look away and walk back to where I left my broom, picking it up from where it fell, and using my pent-up frustration to fuel me. I put all of my attention into the task at hand, letting myself get lost in the push and pull of the broom as I scrub the deck with salty seawater.

At least there's one good thing that will come after all this. I'll sleep like a baby tonight.

Chapter 5

Swim by Chase Atlantic

I expected a bit more of a fight, but I guess being soaked in ocean water and forced to remain in frozen clothes until they dried can take the fight out of anyone.

Aside from Smee, she didn't attempt to speak to the crew the entire day and no one approached her either. Apparently, the passive aggressive grumbling and cursing under her breath was enough warning to keep everyone at bay. No one wanted to have their head bitten off for no reason. Besides, there will be time for introductions and pleasantries this evening.

But I wasn't completely fooled by her outward display of contempt. Without being obvious, I watched her closely. I saw the moments when her eyes kept getting lost on the horizon. Anytime she looked up from the deck, her eyes would drink in the open sky and sea, her eyebrows would relax, and a look of peace would settle on her face. It never lasted long, as if she realized she wasn't outwardly scowling, and she quickly remedied the problem.

Watching her fight so hard to maintain her resting bitch face made me chuckle. I don't know Tink very well, aside from the few times we've interacted in the past, but I'm certain there is far more to her than maybe she even realizes. My certainty only solidified with our interaction in the kitchen.

I stood at the door, transfixed, as I watched her rub that piece of ice on her sun-kissed skin. All tension faded away from her face and body as she completely let go of all pretenses and just existed in the moment. Her short neon green hair was weighed down with sweat and stuck to the sides of her forehead. Her eyes closed, long thick lashes fluttering against her over-heated cheeks, and her luscious pink lips parted in pleasure.

I let my eyes slowly peruse her body, on display in a bright green sports bra and tight, white shorts that should be criminal. She's not overly curvy, but definitely not thin either. The swell of her breasts could still be seen even with the bra constricting them, and her small waist tapered out to hips I could easily grab on to. Her creamy pale skin was flawless, and I wondered if it was as soft as it looked. Then she moaned in pleasure, the soft, sweet sound making my cock twitch, and my eyes snapped back up to her face. I've always thought Tink was pretty in a *come-near-me-and-I'll-stab-you* kind of way, her usual gothic-style clothing and makeup another layer of her *fuck-off* vibe, but I've never really *looked* at her.

Until now.

And fuck me if I didn't love every single bit of what I saw in the kitchen. With her mask of animosity gone, she's actually really fucking beautiful. My nature to tease and be playful is just as engrained in me as Peter's is to be cold and brutal. So, when I turned on the charm to see how Tink would respond, I genuinely couldn't help myself. Not that I wanted too anyway.

And she *did* respond to me. It was an innocent encounter, just testing the waters, but I was delighted to see they may be warm and inviting after all. My only question is, did she respond to *me* or to the situation? I'll have to watch her interactions with the crew before making any more moves, and the way this crew operates, it won't take long for me to figure out her intentions.

Everyone is drawn to sex, to desire, to the feeling of being attractive and wanted. Only, some people want that in the normal sense and others want it in the way my crew does.

Openly and shared.

What does Tink want? There's a spark inside her. I saw it. Hell, I felt it like a match lighting between us. But she's only been one version of Tink for a very long time. She was consumed by Sinful Delights and her obsession with Peter. I can't help the curiosity of seeing who will emerge now that she's been set free from her self-imposed prison. Though, clearly, she sees this ship as her prison and me as her captor. She couldn't be more wrong. In time, she'll come to see that.

For now, I have souls that need my attention. We've docked at The Gates and it's my job to see them through. Jogging up the stairs, I release my wings as soon as I reach the deck. I tuck them in tightly behind me, fighting the urge to spread them wide and launch into the sky. It's the only place I ever truly feel at home.

Home.

It taunts me every time I'm here. Every time I stand literally on the other side of the gateway that will lead me back. I've been in Purgatory with Peter for so long I don't even remember what it was like or what I did to pass the time there. The only memories I have of home are the ones where I was trying to protect Peter from our father's disappointment. Most days, I don't even remember why I'm trying to get back. I just know that it's always been the goal. I was never meant to be in Purgatory, especially not forever.

Smee emerges from below deck, the souls following closely in his wake. Their anxiety rolls off them in waves but there's no sense of fear. These transports are all from dock H1, which means they're all headed to Heaven. Still, this is their final moment of being in Limbo. They're about to enter their final Afterlife and that comes with a lot of unknowns. Hence, the wings. I've learned it helps put them at ease knowing they have an angel guiding them.

As soon as I push all selfish thoughts aside and focus on them, a genuine bright smile splits my face. This is what I do. This is what they need.

"I hope your trip was pleasant and offered you the comfort you needed. Welcome to your final destination! May I present to you, The Gates." I sweep my arm out and gesture to the two enormous arched portals that stand about a quarter of a mile inland. Even in the dim sunlight that clings to the sky, The Gates shine brightly. They're guiding lights that beckon you to them. There's a pull to The Gates that no one can deny, not even those headed to Hell. There's no mistaking them for anything other than Divine.

Collective gasps, along with *oohs* and *aahs*, ripple through the small group of five assembled. I catch Smee's eye, and he winks at me before returning his eyes toward land. There's a smile on his lips but it doesn't quite reach his eyes. He plays it off well but I'm not sure he'll ever completely move on from the fact that he should have been one of the souls crossing over. I'm just thankful to no longer see the memory of his past haunting his eyes. He may not be over his past, but he has found his sense of peace.

Another crew member, Fin, approaches, and nods to Smee before quickly disappearing below deck.

"The gangway is ready, Captain," Smee informs.

"Wonderful!" I boom in a joyous voice. "If you'll all please follow me."

Heading across deck, toward the stern of the ship, I proceed down the gangway knowing Smee will make sure everyone follows as he brings up the rear. The short walk to The Gates is quiet, but it's a light and hopeful silence that fills the space along with my low whistling. Once we reach the fork in the road, I stop and look up at the two portals towering over us.

To the right is the Gate to Heaven. It glows with a pure white light. Heaven's light. It's warm and inviting and calls to me deeply. I can feel the pull towards it like a rope has been lassoed around my torso and gently tugs, urging me forward. I know this is what each of the souls behind me feels too. It's where they belong. It's the call home.

The same will be felt by those heading in the opposite direction. The Gate to Hell is to the left, glowing in a cool, but not cold, blue light. One would think it would glow red or orange to indicate the fiery depths that wait eagerly to torture every soul that crosses over, but that's not what Hell is.

Heaven, Hell, and Purgatory are all different to every single soul. Every soul has a different experience based off the life they lived. That being said, I won't say that Hell is not torturous. It is. Just not always with fire, though that is the reality to some. But no matter what souls face when they pass through these Gates, one thing is certain, they find their peace. Whatever that may be.

I turn to face the souls gathered. "May I present to you, The Gate of Heaven." I gesture to the beautiful, white portal. "I will escort one of you to The Gate, and once you've crossed over, Smee will send the rest of you one at a time to cross. Any questions?"

They all shake their heads and some mutter, "No."

"Very well. Diane," I offer the elderly woman my arm, "shall we?" I smile sweetly at her.

Her wrinkled face lights up as she matches my smile with one just as bright. She nods her head and shuffles toward me, placing her small, delicate hand in the crook of my arm. I place my free hand over hers and lead her down the narrow path toward her Afterlife.

Once stopped in front of The Gate, she tilts her head back, trying to take it all in. "It's the most beautiful thing I've ever seen."

I nod, understanding her awe. "It's nothing compared to what you're about to see."

"I'm nervous," she admits quietly.

She spent last night on deck with me while the others…had

their fun. She had wanted to feel the fresh air on her skin and see the stars one last time, even though I assured her it would not be her last time. I think she just didn't want to be alone. No one does on their final night in Limbo. So, we talked all night. She told me about her husband, Bill, and how they started dating in high school and got married as soon as she turned eighteen. They had four boys and lived a beautiful life together until he died of a heart attack, leaving her to live without him for the past twenty-three years. At the age of ninety-one, she had finally passed peacefully in her sleep.

The reason she ended up in Purgatory is because of her guilt. She remarried after ten years but Bill had been her soulmate, and she was scared he wouldn't be there, waiting for her.

I take both her hands in mine as I turn to face her. "It's just like we talked about last night. Whether Bill is there, waiting for you or not, it will all be as it should. You will be happy. You will find peace. And before you know it, your kids will join you. I promise, Diane, there is absolutely nothing to be nervous about. It will be perfect."

She nods her head, her eyes finally landing on The Gate with renewed determination. "I'm ready."

I lean in and give her a gentle kiss on the cheek. "Welcome home," I say, before letting her hands go and stepping to the side.

I watch as her slow steps take her closer and closer to The Gate. She doesn't hesitate or look back as she steps through, and the white light engulfs her like a familiar, warm, and comfortable embrace.

An immense feeling of comfort settles through me as well. Every time a soul finds their place and accepts it, it's like everything in the world is perfect. In this moment, all is as it should be.

The sound of soft footsteps pulls my attention away from The Gate. "Ah, Christopher!" I beam at the next approaching soul. "Welcome home."

Just like on the ship, I make it a point to spend time with each soul. I take care to remember their names and their stories, assuring them one last time that everything is just as it should be. Once the final soul has crossed over, I finally spread my wings wide and take to the sky. Even though helping these souls cross over brings me a sense of fulfillment and comfort, the fact that I'm always a few steps from home but never able to go back weighs on me.

The Gate has been closed to me ever since I refused to come back immediately after I left. Our father was furious that I chose Peter over him. His punishment for me was locking me out. I haven't tested the portal in centuries. I stopped trying to cross over a long time ago because it never ended well for me. Why continue to put myself through that pain?

Besides, like I said, I don't even remember why I want to go back. I have no idea what would be waiting for me on the other side. Maybe everything. Maybe nothing.

So, I fly.

I let the world fall away from my feet along with all my doubts and pointless thoughts. I push through the clouds just as the sun kisses the horizon and graces me with its colorful beauty. The sun rays and colors are so vibrant and vivid, it feels like I could fly right through them. Like I should be able to feel their weight like a physical touch along my wings.

I continue flying towards the sun until it finally disappears below the sea. The lingering colors of orange, red, and pink slowly start to fade, giving way to twilight when I finally turn back toward the ship. The crew has probably already started cooking dinner, but they won't eat without me so I shouldn't leave them waiting.

Not to mention, Tink is on the ship. She's like a shiny new toy to the crew, and while they've behaved up until now, I know it won't take long before they start to push and press her buttons. I need to be there to make sure they don't take it too far if that's not what she wants.

The image of that ice cube melting along her skin and the sound of her soft moan filters through my memory, urging me to fly faster. I don't know which option I'm hoping for. For her to accept the crew and openly share in their debauchery. Or for her to reject their advances and save all that hidden and pent-up desire for me and *only* me.

"Fuck, what the hell am I even thinking?"

It would make things a hell of a lot easier if she became one of them, but I can't deny the fact that I want to keep this particular little nuisance to myself. For fuck's sake, I don't even know why. Maybe it's the fact that she feels like a challenge, and I haven't had a challenge in way too long when it comes to women.

Speak of the little devil. I spot her bright hair as I fall through the clouds and approach my ship. The sight of her standing on deck sends a shock of excitement racing through me. Maybe I'm no better than my crew after all. I'm reacting this way because she *is* a new, shiny toy on the ship, and I think we're all eager to play. The only thing left to find out is which of us is she going to let have all the fun?

Chapter 6

Moonlit by Rivals

I watch from the top deck as Hook escorts the souls to The Gates.

The Gates.

Talk about a sight.

I've never once questioned my decision to stay in Purgatory. I've never had the desire to move on to anything…*more*. It's like my soul knows its place is here, in Limbo. I've spoken to all the souls like me that have stayed behind and every single one of them has said the same thing; they always feel that nagging sensation in their gut. It fades the longer they stay in Purgatory, and it gets easier to ignore but it never truly goes away. It's like a beacon implanted in your soul, always connected to that one final Afterlife, but I've never felt it.

I thought it might be different standing here now before The Gates, but I still don't feel a thing. They're beyond descriptive words. They're awe-inspiring and so clearly Divine, but that's all they are to me. Something beautiful to look at. There's nothing pulling me toward either one. It's an odd comfort knowing I've made the right choice to stay in Purgatory, but I can't help but wonder why I'm different. Why don't I feel the pull to an Afterlife? Why do I feel like this is exactly where I'm supposed to be?

Those questions are quickly forgotten as I watch Hook take to the sky. Talk about another awe-inspiring sight. I don't know what I expected his wings to look like, I suppose like Sinn's, but his are the exact opposite. They're made of light. Literal fucking light. At least, that's what they look like from here. They're like smoke, twisting and moving but never losing their wing shape. And instead of being black or grey, like smoke, they're white. They remind me of the reflection of water on a wall, and I have the strongest urge to run my fingers through them and find out what they feel like. They look translucent but surely, they must have substance. How else would they be able to carry him?

He disappears above the clouds and the sunset snags my attention, pulling me out of my thoughts. "For fuck's sake, Tink, get your damn head out of the clouds."

Settling against the rail, I let myself get lost in the sky's beautiful display. For so long I kept myself locked away inside Sinful Delights, always wanting to be close to Sinn. Always waiting for him to see me. All that time spent waiting, my eyes laser focused, I never let myself *see* anything else. And the world around me is surprising me in so many ways. My eyes are seeing things in a whole new light, and honestly, it's startling and so damn confusing.

I don't know what to think.

I don't know how to feel.

I feel lost but also like I'm opening up and finding myself. The notion of it all has me internally swaying just as much as the ship has me swaying physically. Instead of feeling any sense of dread or panic, I feel oddly settled.

Swaying and lost and confused, yet settled? I blow out a heavy breath. "I'm a mess," I mutter to myself as I watch the sun sink below the ocean.

It felt like the sun took forever to kiss the horizon, but once it did it was gone much too quickly, twilight lazily making an appearance.

Hook once again falls below the clouds and heads toward the ship. I take a moment to admire the sight once more before I hurry off. I don't know what the hell happened between us in the kitchen earlier but I'm not sticking around to find out. My head is too jumbled to try and make sense of anything at the moment. Instead, I head below deck, intent on locking myself up in my room and avoiding any type of awkward social interaction. I don't really mesh with people, mainly because people are ignorant, selfish, and flat out stupid. My patience and ability to keep my mouth shut are non-existent, so it's best for everyone if I steer clear.

As I approach the kitchen doorway, I hear the murmur of voices and laughter and a delicious aroma makes my stomach growl. I hesitate for a second, looking in on the crew gathered around the large island. The pang in my stomach is almost enough to make me walk inside. Almost. But I don't know the first thing I'd say to these people. I'm the outsider, and I'm definitely feeling the insecurity that comes with it, so I hurry past the doorway.

Before I can make it to my room, Smee comes striding up the narrow hallway toward me. As soon as he sees me, he puts on the charm. An arrogant smirk pulls at his lips and that damn humorous sparkle lights up his green eyes. I immediately roll mine and continue charging forward. I have every intention to push past him, but of course, he blocks me.

"Where do you think you're running off to so fast, little swabbie?"

Little.

Little one.

Little pet.

Little swabbie.

At five feet and not an inch taller, I *am* physically smaller than a lot of people, but that doesn't mean I enjoy being called little. Especially not when I feel anything but little inside. How my small frame manages to contain my attitude is a miracle in itself.

Closing my eyes, I count to five and then let out a heavy, frustrated breath before glaring up at him.

"One, I am not a little anything. Two, you're not my babysitter, or my father, or even my friend, so where I'm going or what I'm doing on my time is none of your damn business."

His smirk widens to a devious grin. "Man, you're feisty. I'm willing to bet you fuck like a wild cat."

I'm surprised I don't give myself a concussion from how hard I roll my eyes. A small part of me likes the attention Smee gives me, but it's a superficial feeling. Every girl wants to feel sexy and desired, but there are levels of realness to it, and I know Smee isn't after me because he's genuinely interested. It's just who he is. A flirt. It doesn't take a genius to figure it out, but I can't help but like the attention. Kind of. Though I refuse to let *him* know that.

"Seriously?" I ask incredulously. "Is that all you fucking think about?"

"Well, when you're good at something…," he maintains his shit eating grin as his eyes slowly rake down my body and back up, "why not do it all the time and share your expertise with others?"

The snort I barely held back a minute ago comes out full force as I cross my arms and pop out a hip, giving him what *I'm* good at. "In my experience, people who feel the need to brag about what they're good at, do it to make up for the fact that they're not *actually* good at it. Those who are let their actions speak for themselves."

He steps closer, his body almost touching mine but not quite. Holding my ground, I crane my neck to look up at him. His height does nothing to intimidate me. I'm used to having to look up at people, and compared to Sinn, Smee is a harmless bunny.

"Why don't you stop playing hard to get and let me show you then? My mouth is good for more than just talking."

A throat clears loudly behind us, making me jump slightly at the intrusion. "Do I even want to know what's happening here?"

Hook's deep voice washes over me and, just like that, my

body is alive and hyperaware of the captain walking up on us. I keep my back to him, still facing off with Smee as a means to distract myself from whatever it is my body is feeling.

"I was just making a generous offer to our new little swabbie," Smee says nonchalantly.

"Generous." I snort again. "Someone as arrogant as you wouldn't know the first thing about being generous. Now, if you'll excuse me, I was just leaving."

His arm shoots out to the opposite wall, blocking me again. "There's really only one way to find out," Smee persists.

I continue looking up at him as I let my eyes go wide and push my bottom lip out in an exaggerated pout. I give him the best fake sad face and voice I can muster. "Oh, boo. Then I guess I'll just never know."

Smee opens his mouth to retort but Hook cuts him off. "Smee."

That's all Hook has to say to silence the cocky chatterbox. I don't need to see his face to know Hook is no longer entertaining this little standoff. His tone of voice leaves no room for argument. Smee's grin falls back to his usual smirk, eyes still gleaming with amusement as he looks me over one last time before giving Hook his attention.

"Captain." He dips his chin and then walks past Hook.

He finally disappears into the kitchen, and I breathe out a heavy sigh, letting my shoulders sag in relief. I hadn't even realized how tense I was.

"He's a pain in the ass but I assure you, he's harmless." Hook's voice snaps me back to where he's standing a few feet away from me. His wings are hidden once again but the sight of him in all that leather, his shoulder-length hair windblown from his flight, is no less arresting.

"Yeah, I know." I shrug, trying to appear just as nonchalant as Smee, but the cool blue eyes watching me closely have me off balance yet again. "I don't need you saving me. I can handle myself."

He chuckles and the sound sinks low in my gut. "Oh, trust me, I know you can. I didn't stop him for your sake but for his. No one wants to deal with Smee if you crush his ego."

"Then he shouldn't put it out there so freely."

"I don't disagree. But enough about Smee, come on. It's time for dinner." He gestures down the hall in the direction of the kitchen.

"I'm not hungry," I lie.

He cocks an eyebrow and continues to watch me closely. Forcing myself to hold his piercing gaze, I hug my arms tighter to my body to keep from fidgeting. I don't like how he looks me. How he seems to see right through me. Compared to Smee's eyes, I feel the realness in Hook's. Maybe that's why it does things to me. Things I don't quite understand. Things I definitely don't want to acknowledge.

"Well then, you don't have to eat, but you do need to meet the crew."

"And if I don't want to? What will you do? Make me walk the plank?"

His bark of laughter is unexpected and makes me feel insecure. I hate when people laugh at me.

"What's so funny?"

"This is a Divine ship that transports souls to their Afterlife, not a pirate ship. Although…," he tugs on his beard contemplatively, "we do plunder for booty."

I remain defiant. "That's not even funny."

"Oh, lighten up, Tink. You *will* meet the crew." His voice has gone hard again with the same tone he used to stop Smee moments earlier. "Unless you'd rather be put on laundry duty."

My eyes narrow. "You wouldn't."

"Funny. You keep telling me what I will or won't do. How did that work out for you last time?"

The memory of Hook grabbing me, pulling me out of bed, and

throwing me over his shoulder replays in my mind. Then his large hand slapping my ass. I was in shock when it happened, but thinking about it now gets my heart racing. Again, for reasons I don't want to acknowledge.

It's Hook's turn to close the distance between us, and once again, I'm left holding my ground, staring up into a handsome face.

"Or maybe that's what you want. Maybe you liked the way I manhandled you. Maybe you want to be thrown over my lap next time." He leans down and whispers the next words hot against my skin. "And spanked until that tight little ass of yours is red with my handprint."

The image he just painted in my mind has my heart racing even faster and I feel my skin heating up. I have to swallow before I can speak, but luckily, I find my voice calm and steady. "Just like Smee, you're delusional. Seems to be a common problem on this ship."

Hook steps back, giving me much needed space. though it still feels like I can barely breathe. "Your words say one thing, your body says another. Around this crew, you should really work on that or else they're going to attack. They're going to sense your desire like blood in the water. They've already been swarming you like the sharks they are, and I've had to keep them at bay. You either meet them now or keep teasing them, making it worse later. Your choice."

"Well, I definitely *don't* want to be attacked in any way, shape, or form, so I guess let's meet the crew, *Captain*." I give Hook my cheesy, fake smile and bat my lashes.

He just shakes his head and turns, walking towards the kitchen, leaving me to follow. I hesitate, not sure what the hell to expect. I already know how *in-your-face* Smee is, and Hook isn't too far off with his observation. Plus, I remember what I stumbled upon last night. A fucking orgy. Yeah, I think I'm allowed to hesitate.

Hook turns to face me when he reaches the doorway, waiting

patiently. I steel my nerves and move forward. Besides, this can't be worse than anything I've experienced at Sinful Delights. I was constantly surrounded by dark, devious souls. This won't be much different than that, I'm sure. I'll just pretend like I'm back behind the bar. Just another night.

When I get to the doorway, Hook gestures for me to enter but doesn't step aside. I have to squeeze between him and the door jam, my body brushing slightly against his. He smirks, knowing exactly what he's doing. I roll my eyes and ignore him as I walk into the kitchen.

Taking a few steps inside, I stop to observe the people before me. There's an ease to the air as they all seem to talk at the same time. A tall, thin woman stands in front of the open refrigerator, her dark-brown hair sleek and straight, pulled into the longest ponytail I've ever seen. When her hair is down, it must pass her ass, easily.

She's talking to a man sitting at the island, but all I can see is part of his profile through the mess of curls that hang around his face as he leans onto the counter, giving her his attention.

Standing at the stove is a man giving Hook and Smee a run for their money in the size department, but all I can see is his broad shoulders and jet-black hair. He's talking to a short red-haired woman that's holding a dish up for him to place food into.

She swats Smee's hand as he walks up and tries to get his hands on whatever is inside. "Get your nasty ass hand out of the food," she scolds. "Who knows where that thing has been."

"Nowhere yours hasn't," he teases back.

Hook clears his throat from right behind me and everyone turns to face us. All talking and teasing immediately stops as everyone's eyes land on me. Great. This is fucking awkward. I knew I should have just gone to my room.

"Everyone, this is Tinkerbell. Tinkerbell, this is the crew. This is—"

A high-pithed squeal cuts him off, and before I know what's happening, a blur of red is charging my way. She barrels into me, wrapping me up in a bearhug that's over just as quick as it started. She holds me at arms-length and beams at me. She's not much taller than I am.

"Oh my goodness! I am so excited to meet you finally! Girl, you are so pretty! I love your hair and your style," she says in a soft, light Southern accent.

She's practically bouncing up and down as she talks, and I'm so thrown off. I'm not sure what I was expecting, but this isn't exactly it.

"Oh, umm…thank you. I really like your hair too. Are those horns?"

She releases me to pat the little horns on her head. "Yeah! Do you like them? They're super easy to style. I could show you if you want. Your hair is a little longer than mine, but I think it could still work."

"Ok. Yeah. Maybe." I smile back at the ball of energy standing before me. It's impossible not to smile when she's beaming so brightly.

"Red, for the love of god, give the girl some space." The other woman says as she moves to sit next to the man at the island.

"How rude of me. Of course, introductions. Well, I'm Red, obviously," she gestures to her bright red hair. Then, she does the exact opposite of giving me space, she links her arm through mine and pulls me further into the kitchen.

"This is Sasha and Fin," she introduces the two sitting at the island.

"Hi," I mumble.

Sasha's deep blues eyes appraise me curiously. They're not exactly warm, but they're not unfriendly either. And wow, is she gorgeous. She's the type of pretty that can not only stop traffic but cause several accidents. If she wasn't an actress back on Earth, I'd be shocked.

The man sitting next to her is more of a kid. He can't be more than twenty-two. His light brown eyes watch me warily. There's uncertainty in them, and when he notices me noticing him, he ducks his head and uses his unruly hair as a shield to hide behind.

Red pulls me up to the island and gestures for me to take a seat. "You can sit by me," she beams as she jumps into the cushy barstool opposite Sasha. "Oh, and I believe you know Smee."

"Unfortunately," I say as I meet his amused green gaze and take my seat.

"It's only unfortunate because you haven't let me worship you yet, princess." He winks.

"Oh, lay off on the charm for two seconds, lover-boy," Sasha interjects. "There will be plenty of time for that *if* she wants it."

"No time like the present," he argues, but shrugs and turns back to the food, now unguarded and up for grabs.

"And last but not least is Killian," Red introduces the man standing at the stove.

He's huge. Not as tall as Hook or Smee, but he's got more muscle than both of them and that's saying something. His lips are set in a thin line, the muscle in his sharp jaw ticks, as if he's angry. A sweep of black hair falls over his forehead but doesn't hide his eyes. Their dark depths meet mine and I instantly feel safe. Everything else about him is big, broody, and intimidating, but his eyes are…amazing. I don't know what it is about them. They're shrewd and calculating. I can see that clearly, and yet, they're also somehow soft and sincere.

"Nice to meet you," he says in a voice that's just as deep and gravely as I expected, then nods his head, and turns back to the stove, breaking our staring contest.

"Well, if you're trying to make me jealous, princess, that worked. Why don't you look at me like that?"

I roll my eyes again. "I didn't look at him like anything, but even if I did, it should be a lesson to you to stop fucking talking. Sometimes, less is more."

"Less is never more with me. You get it all, every hard in—"

"Killian, please tell me dinner is ready and we can eat now?" Red huffs from beside me. "The only time Smee isn't talking is when his mouth is full."

"Everyone loves a full mouth," Smee continues.

"Smee...." Hook's voice demands attention as he moves to take a seat on the opposite side of the island, directly across from me. His large body eases into the seat gracefully and he leans against the back, forearms resting on the armrests. His entire body is relaxed, like I'd imagine a big panther lounging in the sun would be. Meanwhile, I sit up straighter, too aware of the fact that his sea-blue eyes are on me. "Stop being a horndog for two seconds and bring that food over here before you eat it all."

Red reaches for a pitcher in the middle of the island. "Wine?"

I hesitate for a second. The last thing I need is to lose my inhibitions around this group, especially Smee, but it may also be exactly what I need to get through this evening. This is more people than I've been around socially in...well, ever. Add in the fact that *Mr. Sees-Everything* chose to sit right across from me has me two seconds away from bolting like a scared rabbit.

"Yes, please. That'd be great."

Red pours two glasses of red wine and slides one over to me which I accept eagerly and immediately take a gulp of. It's only slightly bitter and leaves a sweet, lingering taste on my tongue.

Smee speaks through a mouth full of food, snagging my attention again as he sets a dish down in the center of the island. "Gotta keep the love machine fueled. Never know when someone will want a ride." He winks at me again.

"My god, does he ever stop?" I mutter softly to Red.

"Oh, princess, that's the last thing you'll be asking me to do when you finally allow me between those pretty legs of yours," Smee practically purrs as he sets another dish down and slides into the seat on my left.

"The only thing these legs will do for you, Smee, is kick you in the balls if you even try to touch me."

Red bursts out laughing, and I earn a quiet chuckle, almost more of a choking sound, from Fin, as if he realized he was laughing and tried to stop it. I give him a small smile before he quickly averts his gaze.

"Oh, I like you," Shasha says with an approving smile of her own. "Anyone who doesn't immediately give in to Smee's attempts is a breath of fresh air."

"He can keep trying all he wants. I'm *never* giving into his attempts."

The amused sparkle is back in his eyes, and he bites his bottom lip seductively before leaning in to whisper in a deep, husky tone. "Challenge accepted, princess."

"For fuck's sake, it's not a challenge." I roll my eyes, but I can't help the smile tugging at my lips, making the gesture less believable. I'm silently grateful for Smee's constant teasing and playfulness. It adds a lightness to the atmosphere that I desperately need.

"Oh, give it up Smee!" Red huffs from beside me, shaking her head.

I take another sip of my wine and feel those heavy eyes on me again. I look up to find Hook watching me, but I can't read him. He's a blank canvas and I find it very frustrating. Especially since he seems to be able to read me like an open book. Even though I don't know what he's thinking, his attention still makes me feel some kind of way. Heat slowly blossoms in my chest, and I don't know if it's from the wine or from him. I lick my suddenly dry lips and the barest flicker of emotion passes through Hook's eyes before it's gone, leaving me to wonder if I imagined it.

Killian sets down another two dishes of food a little harder than necessary, getting everyone's attention and making me jump, quickly breaking my silent staring contest with Hook. He walks away and returns with a stack of plates and silverware. Taking the seat next to Red, he keeps a plate for himself and then hands the others to Red, who takes one, along with silverware, and then passes them to me. I do the same and the stack makes its round until everyone is ready to eat.

Hook closes his eyes and bows his head, obviously saying a silent prayer. I look around and see Killian and Red with their heads bowed as well, but the others just sit quietly until they're finished. It doesn't shock me that Hook says a prayer before his meal, he's an angel after all, but it does surprise me that he doesn't say a prayer out loud and subject everyone to it. Obviously, Heaven and Hell are both real, and as an angel, shouldn't he be trying to sell everyone on Heaven?

As soon as they're done, the silence breaks with a murmur of voices and the clinking of silverware on plates as the food starts to be served. Everyone seems to be talking at the same time.

"Killian, this looks and smells absolutely delicious," Red practically squeals as she takes two pieces of fried chicken from the dish in front of her.

Everyone is reaching for something, but no one gets in each other's way. It's like there's a method to the madness. A routine and comfort in everyone's movements that can only come from so much time spent together. Even the quiet and meek Fin is smiling and chatting eagerly with Sasha. They're not just a crew.

They're family.

A pang of something unpleasant pinches my chest as I watch them. I've never had this. At least, not here in Purgatory. If I had it while I was alive, I don't remember it. Witnessing them interact, their easy laughter and companionship leaves me simultaneously in awe and envious. The cold hard truth about how alone I've been slides over me like ice being pumped straight into my veins.

I thought I didn't care.

I thought all I needed was Sinn.

And without him, I thought I'd be fine on my own. I've never needed anyone before. I've always been perfectly content being a lone wolf. But, if that were true, then why do I feel a huge ball of emotion threatening to choke me? Why are tears welling up in my eyes and threatening to spill down my cheeks?

Just as the first tear starts to spill over, I feel Hook's eyes on me again. I meet his intense gaze but quickly look away and hastily wipe away the tear as I climb out of my seat. Everyone stops talking and stares at me.

"I'm sorry," I mutter. "I'm more exhausted than I realized, and the wine has made me sleepy." I barely lift my gaze off the floor but can't bring myself to look directly at anyone. "Thank you for welcoming me. Enjoy your dinner." I turn and rush out of the room before anyone has the chance to stop me.

"Tinkerbell, wait!"

"Let her go, Red," Hook softly commands.

I run down the hall and throw myself inside my room, practically slamming the door behind me as I lean against it. Once again, I slide down the door and sit lost and confused on the floor. Only this time, it's not shock running through my veins. It's a deep well of emotion I never even knew existed inside of me and it feels like I've been gutted open to expose it.

Ever since I came to Purgatory, I've been an outsider. Yes,

Sinn let me become a part of his team. He has a crew of his own so to speak, but Sinn has never once had a meal with us. We were all just as likely to stab each other in the back if that's what Sinn told us to do. We weren't friends and we definitely weren't a family.

Alone.

I've always been so utterly alone. It's just never been as apparent as it is now. The scenery may have changed, but one thing remains the same. I'm still an outsider. They didn't ask for me to be here. They may try and be kind to me, but I'm not one of them. I'm not a part of their family. I've been forced on them like this life has been forced on me and I've never felt so unsure and insecure in my entire life.

I cradle my head in my hands and do something I can't ever remember doing.

Cry.

Chapter 7

Bleeding Star by Rivals

Well, dinner didn't go as planned. Hell, what was I even expecting? To be honest, I was expecting Tink to be a royal bitch to everyone. I even warned them beforehand that she's cold as ice and not to expect anything other than dirty looks and hateful remarks. I never in a million years expected her to…cry.

I didn't try to hide the fact that I was watching her closely. I wanted to see how she reacted to everyone, especially Smee. I've never cared about his aggressive flirting before. I know Tink isn't anything special to him. Well, she's a challenge. And what is it they say? Not being able to have something makes you want it even more. Smee isn't used to having to try so hard, but he's also not a quitter. He'll continue pursuing Tink until she either gives in or she gets so fed-up she kills the bastard.

I don't particularly want to lose my first mate, but I also don't want to picture them together. When I walked up on them in the hallway earlier, there was a second when something nasty flitted through my body. Something foreign. I wouldn't call it jealousy. There's no reason to be jealous when the crew is open to sharing with each other, but in that split second, I wanted to grab Tink and pull her away from him.

I want to be the first one to touch her.

I want to be the first one to fuck her.

I want to be the one to crack that frozen barrier and make her fucking scream my name to the Heavens for everyone to hear. I want to be the one that imprints in her memory and on her skin long after the marks fade. Then, and only then, will I let Smee and the others touch her.

But at the end of the day, it's not up to me. It's up to Tink. And I don't know how this is going to play out. She acts tough when Smee presses her, but there is that hint of a smile she can't quite hide when he teases her. Does that mean she secretly likes his teasing? And then there's the way her body reacts to me. Is it simply me? Or does she want what any of us can give her?

Attention.

Pleasure.

She may have an icy exterior, but it's thin, and I can already sense it thawing. I thought I had her figured out, I thought I knew exactly how she'd act, but I was wrong. And now I'm second-guessing everything I thought I knew when it comes to her.

"I don't think the counter can get any cleaner."

Sasha's voice interrupts my thoughts and I look down at the stainless-steel countertop I've been wiping subconsciously. We all take turns cooking and cleaning, even me.

"Right." I clear my throat, fisting the paper towel and walking it over to the trashcan so I don't have to face Sasha. Of course, she's not going to let it slide.

"What about her has you all worked up?"

"I don't know what you mean. I was just thinking about the trip back and everything I need to do."

"There's literally nothing you need to do for the trip back. We took care of it when you went to The Gates. You know, *like we always do*," she says sarcastically.

"Right," I repeat. *Fuck's sake, Hook, get your head out of your ass.* Of all the crew members to drift off in front of, Sasha is the only one who'd notice. Maybe Killian, but not to the same degree. Sasha spent her entire life learning how to read people, specifically men.

"I just...wasn't expecting that reaction from her at dinner, that's all. I don't really know how to handle her or this...situation." I don't expand on the situation being that I'm not even sure how to handle my own damn feelings much less how to handle Tink.

"Well, personally, I don't think she's as bad as you let on. I think she tries to act tougher than she actually is. Just give her time to settle and come to terms with everything. In the meantime," she grabs the full plate of food off the island, walks over to me and practically shoves it in my chest, "take this to her."

I clutch the plate to my chest and stare after Sasha as she saunters out of the kitchen, ponytail swaying along with her hips. "Hey! Which one of us is the damn captain?" I yell after her. "I'm the one who gives orders on this ship!"

"Whatever you say, Captain," she chuckles as she exits the kitchen.

My crew have the utmost respect for me, but that doesn't stop them from speaking freely or putting me in my place when I need it, and I wouldn't have it any other way. I'm not like Sinn. I don't want or need people fearing me. Especially not anyone on this ship.

Looking down at the plate of food in my hands, I sigh heavily, and then force my feet to move. I may not have the clearest picture of Tink like I thought I did but I am certain of one thing. She's not going to want to talk to me after she ran out of the kitchen the way she did. She's probably embarrassed and wants to be left the hell alone, but the girl has got to eat.

Taking another deep breath into my lungs, I slowly release it and then reluctantly knock on her door. Silence. Maybe she's asleep. I knock a little louder and then I hear the stir of covers.

"Go away!"

"I just came by to bring you food," I yell back through the door.

"I'm not hungry."

Closing my eyes and gritting my teeth, I mutter to myself, "Lord, give me patience with this one."

Then, squaring my shoulders, I turn the handle. The only light in the room streams in from the now open door but my silhouette blocks out most of it. Good thing I don't need light to see.

Tink is sitting upright now. "What the fuck?! I could have sworn I locked the door."

"No lock on this ship works against me. It's *my* ship, remember?"

"Well, locks are put in place for a reason. To keep people out. I don't care that this is your ship, this is my space while I'm here and I expect to have my privacy respected. So, get the hell out of my room!"

I place the plate of food on the dresser before facing the bed. Tink's small frame is outlined in the dim light, but I don't need a spotlight to show me how angry she is. Or, at least how angry she's trying to be. Her tone doesn't quite have the punch it usually does. It's hard to sound tough when your voice is pinched tight with tears.

Slowly, I move toward the bed and look down at her. The covers are piled around her waist, leaving her upper body exposed. Her arms are crossed under her breasts, pink nipples visible through her thin, white tank top. I watch as they harden under my stare, her chest rising faster than it was just moments ago, but instead of grabbing for the covers to hide herself, she tips her chin up defiantly.

My eyes travel across her collarbone, up the sweep of her neck, to where her lips are pressed into a thin line. Finally settling on her eyes, I see all the mix of emotions I feel reflected back at me. She had still been crying, and I'm not exactly sure what's caused her pain. I've gone over dinner again and again and I can't pinpoint anything that makes sense. No one was mean to her nor was it awkward as I had imagined it would be. Maybe the reality of her situation is finally sinking in and she's crying because she doesn't want to be here. But the tears have now subsided and she's radiating so many other emotions.

Irritation.

Defiance.

Heat.

But most of all, the one I relate to...confusion.

She's just as confused as I am.

Before I even realize what I'm doing, my hand softly cradles her face and I gently wipe her wet cheek with my thumb. She inhales a deep, shaky breath that sounds like a mix of more tears coming and shocked pleasure.

Dropping my hand quickly, I step away from the bed, clearing my throat. "You need to eat. Keep up your strength."

She swallows hard before finding her own voice, more steady and solid now. "I don't need a caretaker and I don't need special treatment."

"I make sure everyone on my crew is taken care of. Trust me, it's not special treatment." I turn and head for the door.

"That's right, you guys take care of *all* each other's needs, don't you?" she says to my back, disgust lacing her words.

I glance over my shoulder. "I expect you up on deck at dawn, ready to work. Don't make me come and get you. I won't be as nice as I was last time."

Before she can reply, I close the door behind me and march straight up to top deck, desperately needing to clear my head. This ship has never felt more suffocating.

Chapter 8

Beep.

Beep.

Beep.

That faraway sound fades again before I can really grab a hold of it. I think my mind is trying to surface memories of my past life, but I've pushed them down and ignored them for so long, they're struggling to be remembered. Besides, dreams are fickle. How do you distinguish between a memory and a fantasy when you can't tell the difference?

Knocking at the door echoes, completely dissolving the dream. Rolling onto my back, I stretch and groan as my entire body protests, every muscle sore from the physical work I did yesterday. Just yesterday, the exact same sequence of events played out giving me an odd sense of déjà vu. It feels like more time has passed than simply twenty-four hours. Maybe it's because I feel like absolute shit from not getting much sleep the past two nights, unable to shut my brain off from driving me crazy.

"Don't make me do this the hard way again, princess. That is, unless you like the *hard* way." Smee's teasing voice comes from behind the door.

I groan again as I push my body up. "I'm up, I'm up. Just…give me a few minutes and I'll head up."

"You have ten minutes and not a second longer. Don't make me come looking for you."

Every ounce of my body and soul wants to lay back down, pull the covers over my head, and try to get some much-needed sleep. If my body wasn't as beat up as it already is, I'd take my chances and do just that, but I don't have the energy to put up a fight today. I don't want to freeze to death again, and I don't want to see what else Hook has in mind if I disobey him again. So, with more determination than I thought possible, I throw the covers aside and climb out into the chilly room

I put on a pair of shorts and another sports bra but also step into a pair of sweats and throw a long-sleeve t-shirt on. At least now I won't freeze in the cool morning air, and I can take layers off when the sun starts to beat down on me. I still don't want to be here but at least today won't be as miserable as yesterday. That's progress, right?

I honestly don't know how long it takes to wash up and head out on deck, but I tried to take additional time to scrub down a bit. After what happened at dinner, I hadn't even thought about showering but am now wishing desperately that I had. Oh well, I'm just going to get ripe again busting my ass on deck today. Besides, who am I trying to impress? It takes way more convincing than I'd like to ensure I'm not trying to impress *anyone*.

Smee is waiting patiently as I climb the stairs and emerge into the fresh morning air, only stumbling slightly as the ship gently rocks from side to side, pushing its way through the waves. When did we leave port? I don't recall falling asleep last night but I also don't remember sensing the ship move.

I immediately feel lighter in the open air, something easing inside of me. My eyes make a quick scan of the deck and notice Hook at his normal post behind the wheel, his long trench coat once again blowing in the breeze and hiding his body.

"The princess emerges, everybody." Smee gestures with wide arms, as if he's addressing an amphitheater full of people waiting for the main event.

None of the crew on deck even acknowledge him and I roll my eyes, prepping for what looks to be a long day of eyerolls.

"Well, I'm here." I lift my arms and let them fall against my sides in a very un-princess-like manner. "What's the chore for today?"

Smee's bright green eyes make their usual path down my body as I come to a stop a few feet away from him. "I have to admit, I liked you better when you were…*wet*. Maybe we should go back below deck and make that happen."

I respond with a deadpan glare. "Smee, I literally just woke up, I'm tired as fuck, haven't had a *sip* of coffee, and I feel disgusting. Not to mention my entire body is sore. Can we not do this right now?"

"Not every part of your body is sore." His eyes look between my legs.

"Ugh." I throw my head back and sigh. "You're so fucking exhausting."

"Just give me a chance, princess. I'll put that ass to sleep."

I look him dead in the eyes. They're sparkling with his normal mischief, but under that, I see the truth of his words. Or at least he believes all the nonsense coming out of his mouth. "You're actually serious, aren't you? Like…really serious."

"As a heart attack."

"Men's egos are unbelievable." I shake my head as I walk past him, his smirk fading when he realizes I am *not* playing this game.

"Hey, where do you think you're going?"

"To wash the deck, I guess. Anything to get away from you," I say, without turning back to face him.

"Hate to see you go but love to watch you leave," he teases as I walk away.

I'm thankful my back is to him and that he can't see the stupid smile tugging at my lips. God, he's insufferable but he also makes everything light and fun with his ridiculous flirting. It's a double-edged blade.

The broom and bucket are waiting for me on the other end of the deck. The familiar and repetitive movements have my muscles screaming, causing me to move slower than I did yesterday. Once my muscles warm up and loosen, they no longer hurt quite as bad. I can still feel the soreness but it's not painful or uncomfortable as I move the broom across the deck.

Push and pull.

Push and pull.

Push and pull.

The simplicity and repetition of the task allows me to free myself from my complicated thoughts. My mind is blissfully blank as I focus on the broom and the deck and nothing else. Before I know it, the sun is high overhead and I'm taking off the extra layer I no longer need.

Humming softly, I continue to scrub the deck until I'm backed up against the opposite end. Only then do I realize I've worked through the entire day. I got so lost in the simple movements, so happy to have my mind unburdened, that it no longer felt like a chore to me. It felt like a reprieve. A break from myself and my reality in the best way.

And not once did Hook, Smee, or anyone else try to interrupt me. Maybe they want to steer clear after I ran out on them at dinner last night. My stomach growls, finally awakening and letting me know that I need to eat. Thank goodness Hook brought me food last night because I wouldn't have gotten any for myself. As much as I complained about not needing a caretaker, it's obvious that I did. Once I stopped feeling sorry for myself, I ate every bite of food on that plate. It's the only reason why I was able to work through the day today and not fall over.

Storing away the broom and bucket, I head to my room for a

change of clothes. I'm in desperate need of a shower before attempting dinner with the crew again. I can smell myself and it's so disgusting. I don't think Smee would even flirt with me right now, that's how bad it is. The thought of Hook seeing me like this, or rather smelling me like this, has me moving faster. I do *not* want that embarrassment on top of everything else. Shower asap. Maybe even a nice soak in the tub to relax my sore and tired muscles.

Somehow, I manage to slip into my room, down the hallway, and into the bathroom without running into anyone. Walking to the far stall, set my clothes down on the bench along the wall, toss my towel over the door, then step into the shower, shutting and locking the door behind me. The space is bigger than I had anticipated, with its own built-in bench against the wall and waterfall showerhead directly in the middle.

Starting the water, I peel out of my sweaty clothes and toss them over the top of the door. Once the water heats up, I step underneath the cascade and immediately moan at how fucking good it feels as the water strips away all the sweat, dirt, and grime. It also feels like I'm washing away the parts of me that no longer fit. As if I'm a snake outgrowing its skin.

It's literally only been two days, but it feels like a lifetime ago. Only two days and I feel like a different person already. Not completely changed, no one changes overnight, but in the process of becoming someone else. Perhaps the someone I was always meant to be. The someone I can discover now that my obsession with Sinn has been ripped away from me.

Moving the loofah across my skin, I wince when I get to my neck. It's still bruised and sensitive from the last time I saw Sinn. I can still feel his hand around my throat, squeezing, and the memory of how his hand felt on my skin still brings me pleasure that I don't completely understand. He was going to kill me, but all my mind could process was his touch. The warmth of his skin against mine. His large body towering over me. His eyes, his attention, on nothing else but me. It didn't matter that it was attention I shouldn't want. I soaked it up. Romanticized it. Made into something that it wasn't.

I grit my teeth against the pain as I scrub harder, trying to erase the feeling of his touch. Anger rises up in my chest. Not at what Sinn did but at what I allowed him to do. Who I allowed myself to become. I lost myself in the pursuit of a man that never wanted me. I made myself into a version I thought he wanted. Someone cold and strong. Someone who could handle him. And when it came down to it, he never noticed either way. He never noticed how much I changed for him. How much I catered to him.

He was my entire world.

"Ow. Fuck!" I whisper yell as the loofah starts to rub my skin raw.

Never again. I will never again allow a man, or anyone, to control me like that. I don't know who I was in my past life on Earth, and I don't necessarily know who I am now, but I'll be damned sure not to let anyone influence who I become ever again. I vow to discover my own truth, to focus on myself, and to hell with everyone else. I may not be the best person, I've made my fair share of mistakes, but no one deserves to be treated like I was. Like I was nothing. Like I was no one.

I am someone.

I deserve better.

I don't know that I'll find my purpose being stuck on this ship but I'm damn sure going to try.

I finish washing my hair and turn off the shower. Grabbing the towel, I dry my hair a bit before wrapping it loosely around my body. I have every intention of soaking in the large tub for a while, so no need to dry off completely. Leave my clothes on the bench, I walk across the bathroom and round the corner, my feet stopping in their tracks as soon as the tub comes into view. I'm standing completely still yet my heart is hammering in my chest as if I just ran a mile.

Hook.

Hook is in the tub.

Hook is *naked* in the tub.

His eyes are closed, head thrown back, resting against the edge. A deep shelf that lines two-thirds of the large tub where it sits in the corner of two walls. Candles are set up in almost every inch of space but none of them are lit, which I am immediately thankful for.

Since he hasn't seemed to notice me, I take my time looking at what I can see of him. My eyes roam over his exposed arms that are resting along the edge. The hints of color I saw beneath his white shirt are now displayed as vibrant ink covering his skin from his wrists, up his defined arms to his broad shoulders, across his massive chest where some of the color is hidden underneath a thin layer of hair, before disappearing beneath the soapy water.

Jesus Christ. This goody-two-shoes, easygoing angel is covered in tattoos. I didn't even know angels could be tattooed.

"Are you just going to stand there or are you going to get in?" he asks without opening his eyes or moving a single muscle. His voice is low and lazy, stirring up my insides.

Fuck. I guess I'm not as inconspicuous as I thought. I swallow down the saliva that's built up from my mouth watering at the mere sight of him. And I haven't even *seen* anything yet. I swear the sound of my heart beating like a caged animal against my ribs can be heard all the way on deck.

The scent of eucalyptus and lavender urge me to toss the towel aside and sink into the steaming water, giving in to its depth, letting it caress my skin and every sore muscle, but my feet stay planted.

"I, uh…I think I'll just go," I say meekly, but my body makes no move to follow my words.

"Get in the water, Tinkerbell." A soft command but a command, nonetheless.

He still hasn't moved, face looking up to the ceiling, eyes closed. I fidget with the towel, my mind running a million miles a minute but not landing on one certain thought. I should go. That would be the smart thing to do. But, if I'm being honest with myself, I don't really want to. I'm done simply *reacting* to situations. Letting men make me feel or do certain things because I think it's what they want. I don't care that Hook told me to get in the water. Before I knew he was here, *I wanted* to soak in the tub, so goddamn it I will soak in the damn tub.

With a new-found confidence that utterly baffles me, I let the towel drop to my feet, then slowly climb into the tub. As expected, the water is perfection. A tad on the hot side but it will feel amazing once my body acclimates to the temperature. My body practically melts as I sink down until the water reaches my chin. I mirror Hook's position and let my head rest on the edge and close my eyes. A soft moan escapes my throat as my body settles, muscles loosening and relaxing.

"Feels good, doesn't it?"

The sound of his voice makes my heart race again. For those thirty seconds or so, I got so lost in the feeling of the water that I forgot he was sitting across from me. I slowly open my eyes, trying to give off the confidence I felt stepping into the tub and not the anxious and nervous version that I actually am.

His turquoise eyes are already on me. Just like the crystal-clear waters of the Caribbean reveal the shadowy dangers down below, his eyes reveal a devious and dangerous thought lurking deep in their depths. He may be an angel but there's nothing holy in the way he's looking at me now.

And it steals the breath from my lungs.

I hold his heated gaze, the air growing charged between us with every electric second that passes. The heat of the water that felt so good moments ago now feels entirely too hot. It feels like I'm on fire, burning up from the inside out. I need to get more air on my skin. I push myself up but stop before the water falls below my breasts. The cool air pebbles my exposed flesh and I shiver, though it does nothing to cool me off.

Hook's eyes darken as they take in my exposed skin but then anger replaces the heat when his eyes rake over my neck. I know there's still bruising there but I have no idea what it looks like after I practically scrubbed the skin off. I have to fight the urge to touch my neck. To duck my head and lower my eyes in shame.

"I don't always agree with my brother's methods. Hell, who am I kidding, I never agree with my brother's methods. Regardless of what took place, that shouldn't have happened." He gestures to my neck.

I shrug, trying to appear indifferent but feeling anything but. The direct mention of it has a heavy weight sinking into my chest, like an anchor, trying to hold me down. "Doesn't matter. It happened, it's now in the past, and I'll never see him again so...." I shrug again.

There's a beat of intense silence filled with words left unsaid before he changes the subject. "I've been watching you."

His confession makes my heart race faster. "I know. Though, I'm not sure why...exactly."

"I know you've seen a little preview of what happens on this ship."

The image of sweaty bodies tangled together, flesh slapping against flesh, moans and cries, Smee fucking that woman while others also got their pleasure, races through my mind. And just like that night, I feel my body responding to the memory. I shift my legs, causing a ripple between us. Hook's eyes drop to the water, as if he can see me clenching my thighs together. Hell, maybe he can.

"And I wanted to see how you would react to it. To the crew."

For the first time since I joined him in the tub, he moves. His arms fall into the water, and he glides in my direction. The giant jacuzzi-like tub suddenly feels way too small as he closes in on me. A shark circling his prey.

His long, normally wild, and windblown hair is slicked back, leaving those beautiful eyes to pierce me as his calloused hands find my ankles, sliding up my calves, making me shiver again. When they get to my knees, he slowly pushes them open. And just like in the kitchen, when he fed me, I let him. My heart is beating faster than I've ever felt, like hummingbird wings that move too fast to see. Even if he can't hear my heart, there's no concealing the rapid rise and fall of my chest.

His hands continue moving higher as his large body squeezes between my legs, until he stops moving, hands resting at the tops of my thighs, lightly digging into the skin.

Still holding my gaze, he continues. "I wanted to see how you reacted to Smee specifically. Do you want to know why?"

I have to swallow again before I can speak. "Why?"

"Because I know the way you react to me, and I wanted to see if it's just the attention and sex you're after." He leans in, putting more pressure on my thighs as he holds himself up, and then whispers in my ear like this is his deepest, darkest secret. "And because maybe I don't want his hands or dick anywhere near you. Maybe I'm the selfish captain who wants to have you first. Touch you first. Taste you first. Fuck you first."

His mouth drops to my sensitive neck, just a faint brush of lips, not quite making contact. His beard tickles against my sensitive skin but the sensation is so much more than skin deep. He pulls back, one hand releasing the grip on my thigh to lift my chin higher, making sure I'm looking at him. His thumb slowly traces my bottom lip as he continues.

"Make that pretty mouth of yours scream my name while those defiant hazel eyes roll to the back of your head as I thoroughly raid your body like a filthy pirate on the seas instead of an angel."

My lips part and I suck in a deep shaky breath, my body shivering once again. An arrogant smirk that could rival Smee's tugs at his beautiful lips. I must look as turned on as I feel, and he hasn't even done anything to me yet. Just the barest touches and heated whispered words have me teetering on the edge of a cliff, more than happy to sacrifice myself by jumping head-first over the edge. Anything to experience more of this feeling swirling inside me.

He pushes away, moving to the side of the tub, and then rises out of the water. The sound of water dripping off his body makes me want to look but I keep my eyes locked forward, staring at the wall as if my life depends on it. I'm not sure how to process what just happened. His admission. And I don't know what it means. After what I saw my first night on this ship, it's clear that the crew does everything together, and I mean *everything*. But Hook said he doesn't want me to sleep with Smee.

He wants to have me.

But again, what does that even mean? He said he wants to have me *first*. He never said he wants me to himself. He just wants to have me first. As if I'm something to be conquered. A prize to be had. He'll have his way with me and then pass me along to the crew once he's done with me.

Fuck that!

I did not just vow to myself to be stronger, to be a better version of myself, just to roll over for another man. I don't care how sexy he is or what his words stirred up inside me.

I deserve better.

I repeat the words in my head like a mantra as my body slowly comes down from the high Hook put it in, trying to ignore how cold I suddenly feel without Hook in here with me despite the water still being warm. I force myself to sink back down into the comforting embrace of the water and try to get back to the relaxed state of when I first got in, but it's pointless. I can't stop picturing Hook's arms and chest or the depths of desire in his eyes. I still feel his fingertips digging into my thighs and his lips and warm breath fluttering softly against my neck. I keep replaying his words over and over again.

And when my hand slides between my legs, I ignore the fact that I'm soaking wet, clit already sensitive and aching for contact. And when my fingers slide inside, I ignore the fact that I imagine it's Hook's fingers instead of mine. And when I cum, I ignore the fact that one name is repeating over and over in my head.

Hook.

Hook.

Hook.

Chapter 9

Give Me A Reason by Versus Me

Heaven above, what the hell was I thinking? Inviting her to get in the tub with me. Her incredible body, naked and glistening mere feet from me. Her skin slightly red from the heat of the water and the sun. The start of tan lines on her shoulders and chest, drawing my eyes to the water, wishing to see more of her body.

And then I had to go and touch her. Her skin as smooth as fucking silk under my hands. The scent of something fresh and citrusy sinking into me, tempting me to put my mouth on her and taste it. I know she was affected by me too, but just how much? The need to drag my fingers across her pussy to see if she was wet was overwhelming. My cock started to harden at the thought, and I had to get the hell out of that tub as fast as I could before I crossed a line I wasn't sure she actually wanted me to cross.

Needing space, I left the ship as soon as we docked. Lord knows I need a fucking distraction and an outlet for my pent-up desire after that encounter with the little viper. There's no better place to find that than Sinful Delights. I'm sure my brother will grumble and question why I'm here again so soon, as if everything revolves around him. Being in charge of this realm, I guess he expects that.

Before pushing through the door, I take a moment to stuff down my frustrations and put on the demeanor he'll expect from me. It's easy to fall into character. After all, there's not much acting involved. I just need to get my mind off Tinkerbell and find another pretty little lady to charm.

"Brother!" I make my way up the ramp to the booth Peter is sitting in, a relaxed stride and an easy smile on my lips as I announce myself.

He never takes his eyes off the dance floor, and I follow his gaze, searching the small crowd. There's a circle around Dee as she sways to the music by herself, content to get lost in the rhythm as if she's in her own little world and not tempting fate if another man even slightly touches her.

Sliding into the booth, I keep my eyes on Dee as I address my brother. "I'm surprised you let her out there on her own."

"Wendee does what she wants," Peter says, eyes still glued to her.

"She sure knows how to put on a show. Aren't you worried someone will touch her?"

"No one would fucking dare," he says through clenched teeth. "And I don't like the way you're watching her, *brother*." His cold eyes finally address me.

Deep blue arctic eyes; a stark contrast to mine. We are the exact opposite in every single way, but I still love him like no other. He's my blood. My little brother. And I've always felt the need to protect him, even though I failed at every turn.

Chuckling, I blatantly ignore his threat. It doesn't mean shit to me. I know he's overly protective of Dee and would keep her locked away in his penthouse if he could, so I don't take the threat personally.

"Well, I see nothing's changed then. You're still a miserable bastard."

"What are you doing here, Hook?" he asks, taking a long swig of his bourbon.

"What am I always doing here, brother? Getting a drink and having some fun. I can't let you be the only one getting some pussy."

"Speak like that about Wendee again and I'll—"

"Hook!" Dee's excited voice cuts him off as she comes trotting up the ramp. I barely manage to step out of the booth before she's wrapping me up in a bear hug that elicits a dangerous growl from Peter.

"Oh, for Christ's sake, Sinn, knock it off," Dee laughs easily as she releases me. "You have no reason to be jealous and you know that."

"I'm not *jealous*," he hisses, pulling her in close to his side as she climbs into the booth. "I'm possessive. There's a difference." He grabs her chin roughly and jerks her face up to look at him. "No one else should ever feel that gorgeous body pressed against them. It's mine to feel and *only mine*. You're going to pay for that later." He nips at her bottom lip, and she moans, sinker further into him.

I clear my throat. "Well, good to see some things haven't changed. You're both still disgustingly in love I see."

Though I'm only teasing. I never thought I'd ever see the day Peter fell in love and I couldn't be happier for them. He's still the cold and dangerous Angel of Death that people fear, but I know behind closed doors Dee gets to see a side of him no one else ever has or ever will. Not even me.

"What are you doing here so soon, Hook?" Dee asks sweetly, despite the grumbling Peter gives her. "Was an escape needed that badly?"

"That obvious, huh?" I chuckle again.

"I don't know how you're going to manage it. I'm sorry she's been thrown on you. I wish there was another option."

"If anyone can handle that traitorous little bitch, Hook can," Peter says confidently. "After all, aren't you always boasting about how you can charm *any* woman?"

The image of Tink in the kitchen rubbing ice over her heated skin, then looking up at me as I hand-fed her flashes through my mind.

And all too fresh in my mind is the tub. I can still feel her skin under my hands, her scent invading me, legs and lips parted for me as her chest rose and fell, revealing the swell of her breasts above the water as I told her I want to fuck her. There wasn't an ounce of resistance or repulsion in her eyes. My cock twitches at the mere thought of sliding into her for the first time. She's definitely a fucking problem, just not in the way they think she's a problem.

A bucket and glass being set down in front of me rattles me out of my thoughts. I clear my throat again and school my features into the charming playboy. I don't know what emotions just revealed themselves and I'm grateful for the distraction.

"Ah, my favorite bottle of rum!"

"Yes, I remembered from last time." The shy waitress blushes and barely meets my eyes before looking down at the table again.

"That's right. Tillie, is it? No," I continue before she can say anything. "Millie. It's Millie, isn't it?"

Her blush deepens and she nods her head.

"Well, Millie…." I take her hand in mine and pull her closer until I can tip her chin up to look at me. The motion has me back in the tub with Tink, big hazel eyes looking at me instead of Millie's blue ones. I have to shake my head to dispel the image. "Once I'm done here, how about I come find you?"

She bites her lip and nods again, voice barely above a whisper. "I'd like that."

Placing a chaste kiss to her knuckles, I let her go. She hurries off and I pour myself a much-needed glass of alcohol. I want to throw it back and immediately pour a second, but I refrain. Instead, I take an easy sip and lounge back in the booth, the picture of comfortable ease.

"You were saying?" I smirk at my brother, who just grunts and drinks his bourbon.

Dee laughs heartily and steals my attention. She asks me

questions about everything. What it's like to be out on the sea. What The Gates are like. How many crew members I have, and how they came to be on my ship. She's easy to talk to and keeps me distracted from my thoughts about Tinkerbell until my exasperating brother decides he's had enough of sharing Dee and steals her away. Of course, she's all too eager to follow behind him as he leads her to the elevator.

Pouring one last glass of rum, I gulp it down before deciding what my next move is going to be. Almost the entire bottle is gone but I'm barely feeling the effects, my damn angel blood not allowing me to succumb to it like humans can. The only reason why Peter and I drink is because we enjoy the taste of it, the burn of the alcohol as it slides down your throat and into your chest. Only, that feeling dissipates and never fully pulls us under. The nagging feeling in my chest right now has absolutely nothing to do with the rum.

I contemplate seeking out little meek Millie and giving her the second-best night of her life. Can't say it would be fun, but it would at least take the edge off. Closing my eyes, I imagine her petite body beneath me as I slide in deep, a gasp escaping from her sweet mouth as heated hazel eyes lock with mine.

"Fuck," I mutter as I slide out of the booth and head back out the way I came.

The walk to the docks is fairly quiet, only a few souls milling around, always drawn to the docks for reasons they don't fully understand. All too soon, I'm standing on the dock staring up at the Jolly Roger. From the outside, it doesn't look like anything special. Just another ship. But that's the illusion. No one is supposed to know it's a Divine vessel until they're ready to make their journey to The Gates.

I hesitate before stepping any closer. I'm not sure why this thing with Tink feels different. Maybe it's because I know her. Well, in a way that one knows an acquaintance, but still more than I've ever known the souls that end up on my ship for transport. She's been a part of Sinful Delights for a very long time. She's also been chasing after Peter for a very long time. Perhaps that's why I've never seen her as anything more before. But now....

Fuck. What about now?

Honestly, what's changed? It's only been a couple of days. She's probably still thinking about my brother every two goddamned seconds. There's never been competition between him and I. We've never acquired the same tastes but a part of me wants to claim Tinkerbell as mine and only mine. Is that because Peter has Dee? Do I want what he has? It's never been my focus before. I love the dynamic I have with my crew but another part of me doesn't want to see Tink become like them. Why?

A gentle breeze kicks up, lightly blowing through the strands of my hair. Closing my eyes, I relish the feel of it and let the familiar scent of the ocean settle me. Until I smell the other scent on the breeze.

Sex.

"Fuck," I curse under my breath, the nagging feeling back in my chest as my feet finally move.

There's no more time for hesitating and driving myself mad on a merry-go-round of confusing thoughts. New souls won't board until tomorrow, until they're ready for transport, which means the crew are having their fun together.

With Tink.

The thought has me sprinting up the gangway, across the deck, and down the steps at record speed. Once I make it below deck, I stop for a moment to listen, getting the location of the crew. The sounds are coming from the direction of Red's room.

The hallway is shrouded in darkness, but I can see clearly. It doesn't take me long to spot Tink hiding in the shadows, standing in the middle of the hall, eyes glued to the open doorway. Her chest is rising and falling quickly, but other than that, she's standing as still as a statue. I'm certain she doesn't want to be seen spying, although the crew would only welcome it.

Welcome *her.*

Immediate relief floods through me knowing she's not in the room with them. No one else has touched her. Kissed her. Fucked her.

Keeping my movements slow and steps silent, she never hears me approach until I'm standing a few feet away from her. "Well, well. What do we have here?"

She jumps, slapping her hand down on her mouth to stifle the yip of surprise.

Stepping even closer, I whisper, "Look who enjoys watching."

Once she regains control of herself, she lowers her hand and whispers back, "What? No, I don't. I...I was...it's not—"

"Smee is good at what he does," I interrupt her. "And he loves to put on a show. They all do. Even shy Fin has become fond of the attention. There's no shame in enjoying it."

She shakes her head emphatically, eyes wide in shock. "It's like a car wreck. You don't want to look but can't look away, that's all. I wasn't *enjoying* it."

Reaching out slowly, I gently trace the line of her sports bra, feeling the swell of her breasts. "Then why are you breathing so fast?" I place my palm flat against her chest, feeling her heart pound like a battering ram. "And why is your heart beating so hard?"

She opens her mouth to argue but no words come out.

I step in closer, sliding to stand directly behind her. God, she's so incredibly small compared to me. I have to practically bend in half to whisper in her ear. "The pulse in your neck, pounding wildly with anticipation."

My fingertips move to her bare shoulders, slowly grazing her skin as they make their way down her arms, goosebumps following in their wake. They trail down her hands and land on her thighs, touching bare skin again, exposed in another pair of tight, barely-there shorts.

"And your thighs clenching with desire." She shivers as my fingertips slowly make their way to the inside of her thigh.

Only this time, I don't stop. My fingers slide over her shorts and down the middle of her pussy, testing the line between us. I'm still not entirely sure if I should cross it but I'll let her decide. I move slowly, giving her ample opportunity to pull away or tell me to stop. As I start to gently rub her clit, she inhales a shaky breath and spreads her legs wider. That's all the invitation I need.

Wrapping my left arm around her waist, I tug her backwards until my back is up against the wall and she's pressed firmly against my body. I rub her clit over her shorts in soft, slow strokes. Keeping my voice low, I continue to talk to her, drawing her attention back to what's happening inside the room.

"Look at Sasha," I demand. "Isn't she beautiful? The way she gives all her attention to Fin, making him feel like he's the only person in the room. Look at the way she holds his gaze. The way she moves her body to meet his strokes, taking him harder, deeper. The way her arms and legs cling to him like he's her life saving buoy, and if she lets go, she might drown."

Her chest is rising faster now, her body radiating heat where it's pressed against me. She's still a bit tense, as if she's not entirely sure how she feels about what we're doing, but she still hasn't told me to stop.

"Or maybe you like what the others are doing more? Do you like watching Red take Smee's cock down her throat while Killian fucks her from behind?"

She swallows hard, practically panting, but she still doesn't say a word. I move my hand up to the band of her shorts and slide underneath them, finding no panties to get in my way. A deep rumble of approval fills my chest, and my dick starts to harden. When my fingers slide down the middle of her pussy, she finally lets out a strangled moan and lets her head rest against my chest.

"Mm," I groan as my finger slides inside. "You do enjoy watching, little viper. You can deny it all you want but this tight little pussy says different." I pull my finger out of her and slide it over her swollen clit. "Feel how wet you are. That's from watching the crew fuck each other, isn't it?"

When she doesn't answer, I pinch her clit. She barely manages to stop the cry of pain from escaping her mouth.

"Isn't it?" I ask again in a low growl.

"Yes," she finally admits, her voice low and shaky.

"That's a good girl."

I reward her by rubbing her clit again. I continue to slide my fingers between soaked lips, gathering her wetness and coating her clit as I continue to rub it in slow, deliberate circles. Her citrus scent is now laced with her desire and I'm dying to have a fucking taste. To bury myself between her legs and let her juices coat my lips, tongue, and beard. Instead, I continue to hold her against me, continue to let her watch the show before us while I focus solely on her.

Pressing my hips forward, I let her feel my own arousal so she doesn't feel like she's alone in this.

"Do you feel how hard you've made me?" I press harder on her clit, and she moans, no longer as quiet as she was. Her hips rock against my hand, seeking pleasure. "Because I can assure you it's not what's happening in that room that has me hard. I've seen this show more times than I can count. It's you. The little poisonous viper caught in my grip, at *my* mercy." I leave her clit to push two fingers inside her, pumping them in and out, matching her rhythm as she pushes her hips forward, asking for more. When I find her clit again, I'm done teasing.

I use three fingers to rub across her clit almost frantically.

"Oh, God," she breathes out, voice airy and light. A tone I've never heard from her before but want to hear again. And again.

Her body is trembling against me, legs shaking and threatening to collapse. I wrap my arm tighter around her waist, holding her up.

"There's no God here, no Devil, and no Angel of Death, just your Captain. And *I'm* the one that's going to make you cum."

Almost before the words even leave my mouth, she clamps both hands down over her mouth as the orgasm hits her. I keep rubbing her clit even though she's now trying to move her hips away from me. She has nowhere to go as I draw out her orgasm.

Her cries are held hostage in her throat, and I want her to set them free. I want to hear her beautiful voice as it screams and cracks from the pleasure.

Her body convulses against me as the orgasm fades. Little uncontrollable spasms that rock through her body until her knees give out and she slumps in my arms.

Removing my hand from her shorts, I bring my fingers to my mouth and make sure she hears me sucking them clean. "Mm, who knew sour little Tink could taste so fucking sweet."

She finds her footing and clears her throat, finally pulling away from me. When she turns to face me, barely meeting my eyes, I start to second-guess everything we just did. Maybe she didn't really want this to happen after all and I forced it on her. Maybe she was just caught up in the moment, everything happening around her, and now she regrets it.

Fuck.

Before she can say anything, I save ourselves both from the awkward embarrassment. "Goodnight, Tinkerbell." I push off the wall and begin walking down the hallway toward the bathroom.

She may regret it, but I sure as hell don't. All I can think about is how can I do it again? How can I get her to say yes, for real this time? Did I already fuck that chance up?

Fuck.

I barely pull my clothes off before barreling into a shower stall and turning on the cold water. The water pelts my heated skin, cooling me down on the outside but unable to do anything about the fire in my gut. Taking my hard cock in my hand, I stroke it with all the pent-up frustration inside me, needing it hard and on the verge of pain. Anything to take the edge off. The only fucking problem is there's only one thing that's going to satisfy me now.

Tinkerbell.

Chapter 10

Better Way Out by Caskets

When the light of dawn starts to filter in through the window, I'm already wide awake. What happened last night replays on a non-stop loop in my mind. And not just what I saw this time.

What I did.

What I allowed Hook to do.

I let him touch me. I let him make me cum. And although I didn't have much sex at Sinful Delights, I'm far from a virgin. I know how sex makes me feel, which is only slightly more than how I normally feel.

Numb.

Empty.

Disconnected.

Sex has never brought me the type of pleasure Smee seems eager to show me. I don't have the same need to have sex like they do on this ship. At least, I didn't. Hell, I don't know what I feel now. I just know that how I feel on this ship is different than anything else I've ever felt before.

Watching the crew have sex, seeing how much they all enjoy it, how...*engaged* they all are, is unlike anything I've known before. My experiences have been nothing like that. Mostly, they've been about the guy getting off in two minutes, leaving me asking myself what the fuck was the point.

And how I feel around Hook....

Fucking hell. It's like I've been walking around as a ghost for a hundred and fifty years; never seen, never noticed or heard, and now I'm standing front and center in a spotlight. When Hook looks at me, I feel seen. And when he touches me, I swear I'm alive. My body ignites in ways I've never felt before.

He barely touched me last night and I melted in his arms. Just a few minutes of his skilled fingers sliding inside me, rubbing against my clit, and I was utterly helpless. And when he said he was hard because of me, letting me feel his arousal…fuck. It made my chest swell and head swim.

His touch, his voice, his body pressed against mine, was all I could think about as I lay alone in my bed, aching for more. And when I finally fell asleep, he followed me for a repeat performance in my dreams. I woke up on the verge of cumming again, just from the fucking dream!

The only thing stopping me from sliding my hand under my shorts the same way he did is the knock on my door that I'm sure is going to come any second now. As if I manifested it, the knock echoes right on cue.

Sighing heavily, I push the covers off me and slide my legs over the side of the bed. "I'm up, Smee, I'm up!"

"It's Red!" Her excited voice filters through the door. "I was hoping I could come in?"

As much as I may want to open up to these people, it's not easy to change who I am overnight. I'm not used to anyone ever *thinking* about me, much less wanting to…what? Hang out with me?

"I have pancakes and bacon," she singsongs in a bribe.

Walking to the door, I open it a crack and peer out, still hesitant, and unsure it's not some nasty trick from Smee to get me up. Sure enough, Red is standing in the hallway in a black silk robe with two plates stacked high with pancakes and bacon. The exuberant smile on her face is impossible to ignore and I can't help the small smile that pulls at my own lips.

"Well, why didn't you say so sooner?" I open the door wider, allowing her in.

She squeals in delight and practically skips into my room. "I knew it! You can never go wrong with pancakes and bacon. You've got to be a complete weirdo not to like pancakes and bacon."

She sets the plates down on the bed, climbs under the covers and pats the bed next to her before reaching for the plates again. She's inviting me to sit in my own bed as if it's hers. Hell, I guess this ship is more hers than mine.

I reluctantly walk back to the bed and take a seat next to her, propping myself up against the headboard like she did. Once I'm settled, she hands me one of the plates.

"I know you're not used to the crew yet, and trust me, I know how exasperating Smee can be." She rolls her eyes but there's no real annoyance behind the gesture. It's clear that this crew is a tight-knit group. "But he's harmless, truly. We all are," she insists as she meets my eyes. "But I'm the most recent to the group, so I know how it can feel being the outsider."

"Something tells me you've never been an outsider, Red. At least, not for long."

"That's true," she laughs around a mouthful of pancake. Once she gets it down, she shrugs, and the bright smile is back. "I can't help it. I just love getting to know people."

"Well, that makes you the exact opposite of me," I admit before taking a huge bite of pancake. "Oh my god," I mumble around the food, hiding my mouth with my hands.

"Pretty great, right?" she beams.

"Great?" I stare at my plate as if I've never seen pancakes before. "These are the best things I think I've ever tasted."

She swallows another mouthful, nodding. "Get used to it. Everything Hook makes is, for lack of a better word, divine." She laughs as she picks up the bacon and takes a bite. "I bet everything that man does is divine," she says with a daydreamy sigh.

I study her as I take another bite, remembering what I watched last night, and quickly following that memory is the memory of Hooks fingers sliding between my legs. I practically choke on the pancakes this time and it doesn't take long for the heat to flush my face.

I clear my throat and try to play it off. "I, umm…." I bite my lip and busy myself with cutting another piece of pancake. Anything not to have to face her as I admit I was watching them like a creep. "Well, last night. I, uh…."

"Oh, did you hear us? Sorry, we tend to get a little loud sometimes."

"No, I…well, yes, I did hear you. But I, umm…I also sort of…*saw* you guys." I glance up, waiting to see her shock or embarrassment, but she doesn't seem fazed at all.

"Oh, yeah. We don't really shut doors around here either. You'll see us more often than not, I'm sure. Heck, Smee is dying for you to join us."

I must look as utterly shocked as I feel because one look at my face has her back-pedaling. "Oh goodness, I'm sorry if that makes you uncomfortable. I forget that not everyone is as open as we are." Her shoulders slump and a frown tugs at her lips. "I'm sorry."

She looks devastated and I'm not sure why, but I hate it and immediately want to fix it. "No, no, it's totally fine. I don't mind. I mean, this is your ship, your home, you guys can do whatever you want on it. It's just…new to me, is all. I'm just…*really* not used to it," I laugh nervously.

"I totally get it! I was pretty shocked when I first got here too, but it faded quickly for me. I don't know, something about this crew is just…," she shrugs again, "special. It was a no brainer for me to stay."

"How long have you been a part of the crew?"

"Not that long, honestly. Only about five years, but it feels like I've known them forever." She smiles brightly again. "It was an instant connection, at least on my end, and I'm grateful that they welcomed me with open arms."

"And open legs," I mutter before I can stop myself.

She covers her mouth so she doesn't spit food everywhere, but as soon as it's down, she throws her head back and laughs. "Touché, girl. Touché. Though it took me a while before I got to that point with them, so I get it. Sasha actually helped me a lot."

There's one question in my brain that is screaming to be asked but I'm trying not to sound overly interested or crazy, but I need to know.

"So, Hook…," I start, "he, uh…he's ok with what you guys do? I mean, obviously he is, and not that there's anything wrong with it," I add quickly.

"Oh yeah, he's fine with it as long as what happens on this ship stays on this ship. He'll join in for some fun once in a while with souls we transport but he's never been with anyone in the crew, much to our disappointment."

"He hasn't?" The question comes out a little too quickly. Luckily, she doesn't seem to notice.

"Uh-uh," she shakes her head. "He has most of his fun at Sinful Delights when we dock. He says since we don't get to leave the ship and he does, that he'll leave the souls to us to have our fun with. If they want, of course."

"Of course," I answer automatically, but my mind is still stuck on the conversation we had in the tub. I can still hear his whispered confession, still feel his hands on my skin.

And because maybe I don't want his hands or dick anywhere near you. Maybe I'm the selfish captain who wants to have you first. Touch you first. Taste you first. Fuck you first.

If he's never been with any member of his crew sexually, then why me? What makes me different? But maybe I'm not. Not really. He kept repeating the word *first*. He just wants to claim me. It reminds me of a dog lifting its leg up to mark its territory. The thought just pisses me off. And to think, I almost let him!

In fact, as soon as he was done with me in that hallway, he left. He just fingered me like it was nothing and fucking left. I was so caught up in his words, thinking that I was something special, when all I am is the shiny new plaything on the ship. He doesn't want anyone playing with me until he's done with me.

"That fucker."

"What was that?"

I snap my head up, noticing Red watching me intently. I hadn't meant to say that out loud. "What?" I shake my head. "Oh, nothing. It was…nothing. So, why is it past dawn and I'm still in this bed, eating breakfast? I was sure it was Smee coming to get me when you knocked."

"There's nothing to do today. We already stocked up on supplies when we were here a couple days ago. Now we're just waiting for the new souls we'll be transporting to be ready. They usually board in the afternoon or evening, so we have most of the day to just relax."

"Oh. Ok."

"This really is a good gig. I promise you won't be washing the deck forever. I mean, you will, but we all take turns. We take turns doing everything. Even Hook washes the deck. They just want you to think it's the grunt work as the newbie to get you in line." She grimaces. "Please don't tell them that I told you."

I smile at her. "I won't, I promise."

"Oh, thank you!" She releases a heavy sigh.

We both nibble on the rest of our food, but our minds seem to be somewhere else as the silence stretches between us. I'm frustrated that my mind still seems to be stuck on Hook.

"Can I ask you a personal question?" Red interrupts my thoughts. "You don't have to answer if you don't want to."

I nod. "Ask."

"Why are you here?"

"Like on this ship or in Purgatory?"

She shrugs. "Both?"

I shake my head. "No big mystery to any of it. Well, I guess that's all there is as to why I'm here, in Purgatory. I don't know. But I'm on this ship because I betrayed Sinn."

"Sinn?" Her eyes practically bulge out of her head. "As in the Angel of Death? As in Hook's brother?"

I nod again. "It's a long story. The short of it is, I tried to force the woman he loves into her Afterlife. I thought I was doing it for him. I mean, in the moment, I was so sure I was but...."

"Now you're not so sure?"

"Now I'm not so sure of anything."

"What do you mean?"

"I thought I loved him."

She gasps. "Sinn?"

I chuckle. "I know, frightening, isn't it?"

"I mean, he helped me find my unfinished business, which I'm grateful for but...yikes! I can't say I'd want to be anywhere near that man on my own volition."

"He never scared me like that," I admit. "I don't know, I just always thought there's got to be more to him than what he shows on the surface, ya know? And there is. He just never chose to show me."

I scoff. "A hundred and fifty years I was by his side and not once did he ever glance my way with the hint of anything more in his eyes. Just once, I wanted him to see me the way I saw him but…."

"And now? You don't think you loved him after all?"

"How can that be love?" I ask, looking in her eyes. "The man barely tolerated me on a good day, but I never saw it. Not like I do now. I was just so caught up in what I wanted, what I hoped for, what I imagined, that I totally and completely lost myself to it. To the fantasy that if I just waited long enough, if I could just be who he wanted…." The shame I feel at admitting this out loud rocks through me. "It took being forced from his side for me to finally gain clarity, but the only things I'm sure of is that it definitely wasn't love, and I don't even know who I am."

I can't help but also think about how much my body reacts to Hook. If I loved Sinn like I thought I did, wouldn't I be unfazed by another man? That's what love does. It makes you utterly blind to anything and anyone else.

"Well," Red pulls me out of my thoughts again, "you can be anyone you want to be here! Treat this like your fresh start! No one here knows who you used to be, so if that's not who you want to be anymore, then don't."

I huff. "You make it sound so easy."

She shakes her head. "Not easy, but possible. And I'll be here to help you. So will the rest of the crew if you want them to. Just like they helped me."

"What about you? Why are you here?"

She sighs heavily before I watch her steel herself against the memory. I immediately feel guilty for asking. Tipping her chin up, she meets my eyes. "I was molested by my stepfather. It started when I was eight, just touching me more, sitting me in his lap, that kind of thing. Naturally, it progressed over time. I told my mother, but she didn't believe me. When it finally got to the point where he was having sex with me, there was no denying it or hiding it. I know she could hear him in my room, hear my crying, but still, she never said a word to stop it. One day I snapped. I grabbed a knife from the kitchen and attacked him. My mother actually tried to stop me," she laughs sarcastically. "Can you believe that? So, I killed her, too."

"Oh my god, Red. I'm so sorry." I don't even think about it, I just reach over and grab her hand. She takes it and I squeeze, giving her all my attention and as much support as I can as she continues.

"I was only fourteen when I killed them. I went into a juvenile detention center and was released when I turned eighteen. I was told I could go out and continue to live my life how I always wanted to, as if what I went through hadn't seriously fucked me up. I'm honestly lucky to have lived as long as I did. I got into a car accident on my twenty-sixth birthday and died. I ended up here because of the guilt I carried for killing my mother. I was headed for Hell when I decided to stay here, with Hook and the crew. It's the only good decision I've ever made besides killing that motherfucker."

I tilt my chin up too, mirroring her determination and strength. "You did what anyone in your position would do. I'm sorry you went through that and I'm sorry you had to carry that guilt. It's not fair."

"No, it isn't, but life rarely is. Being here, I get to meet so many people, get to hear their stories, and honestly, it's the best life I think anyone could have. As sad as it is, you get to hear the most awful stories, but it helps you feel less alone in the world. And you get to hear some of the best stories that help you see the rare beauty in an otherwise ugly world. This ship, this crew, and Hook really are the best things that have ever happened to me, and I know I'm exactly where I'm supposed to be. Everything that happened in my life led me to right here."

"I admire your courage and strength, and I envy your

certainty." I smile weakly.

"You'll get there too. I just know it." It's her turn to squeeze my hand.

"Well, that makes one of us."

"So, all this time here and Sinn was never able to help you find out why you're here?"

I shake my head. "He said whatever I experienced in life, I didn't want to face. Apparently, I'm the one blocking my own clarity, though I have no idea how to even stop. At this point, it honestly doesn't even matter. It's been so long."

"It does matter. And I'm here for whatever you need." She squeezes my hand and I squeeze back.

The resolution is clear in her eyes. She means what she says. This complete stranger, who lived through one of the most horrific things I've ever heard, is one of the brightest and kindest souls I've ever met. I'm not worthy of her kindness, but a selfish part of me wants to accept it anyway. The reality is I've never had a friend before. I don't know how all of this works and the emotion I feel blossoming in my chest is threatening to choke me.

Just as a tear slips down my cheek, I'm pulled into a hug. My immediate reaction is to pull away, but Red's words sink into me.

You can be anyone you want to be here! Treat this like your fresh start! No one here knows who you used to be, so if that's not who you want to be anymore, then don't.

And I don't want to be the person I have been for as long as I can remember. I don't want to be the girl who lost herself trying to be someone else for a man that never even noticed her.

I don't want to be cold.

I don't want to be angry.

I don't want to be detached.

I don't want to be…alone.

So instead of pushing Red away, I hold on tighter and let the tears run down my cheeks. Tears that feel like letting go. Tears that feel like starting over. Tears that feel like I finally have hope instead of hopelessness.

"Thank you, Red," I whisper into her shoulder. "Thank you."

Chapter 11

Today was completely unexpected. I spent the entire morning lying in bed with Red. I was dying to ask her about the rest of the crew, to hear their stories, but after our heavy conversation, we kept it light and fun. I've never had a girlfriend before but Red makes it easy to warm up to the idea. I haven't laughed so much since…well, ever.

There was the slightest inkling of familiarity, as if I had in fact, had a girlfriend before but the feeling was fleeting. Whatever life I lived when I was alive still remains hidden to me. For the first time, I find myself wanting to remember. I want to know who I was before I turned into *this* version. Was I always this way? Or was I more like Red? I feel like I can't truly be who I want to be now without knowing who I was in life. I don't want to just decide to be someone new. I want to be who I was, or at least a better version of that.

I want to know my truth.

My new resolve has me feeling more grounded than ever as I stand on deck watching the new souls board. There are only three this time, two men and one woman. As they're led across deck by Smee, one of the men looks my way. The glint in his eyes makes me shiver despite the late afternoon sun shining down on me. I have the urge to glare at him and flip him off, but another idea sparks in my mind, so instead I give him what I hope is a promising smile. He winks at me before following the others below deck.

Blowing out a nervous breath, I move to the rail and look out over the city. I can't see Sinful Delights from here but the longing to be back there is strong. Despite my feelings for Sinn, whatever they may or may not be, that place is all I've ever known. It's home. Or at least, it was.

"Is it hard to be back here so soon after you left?"

I glance to my left to see Sasha mirroring my pose against the rail. "I didn't leave, I was *forced* to leave," I bite out, immediately regretting my quick, angry response.

"Then it must be even harder to be back," she says matter-of-factly, no pity in her tone.

"It is. It's the only place I've ever known."

"I can see how that would make this difficult but it's also a hindrance."

I turn to face her. "What do you mean?"

"There's more to life than one place, one outlook. If one place, one life, is all you ever know, then how can you ever hope to grow?" She levels me with fierce, intelligent blue eyes. "You can't," she answers before I can. "You stay stagnant, comfortable, and even unknowingly ignorant. Change is a good thing, as long as you're open to seeing it as positive instead of negative. You're in control of how you react to this new life whether you chose it or not. I hope you're open to seeing the possibilities that are clearly right in front of you."

Before I can even process her words much less respond, she walks away, leaving me with my jaw on the deck. It's basically the same advice Red gave me, just way more blunt-and in-your-face. Hell, it's what Hook has been trying to get me to understand this whole time, too. This is going to be as easy or as hard as I make it. The one thing everyone seems to be telling me is, I am in control.

It's such an odd concept for me though. I've never been in control before. I've always been under Sinn's control. I've always had to do what he said, when he said. Not that I ever cared before. I had no problems being that person until Wendee showed up. That was the first time I'd ever acted on my own. If you would have asked me three days ago, I would have said it was the one and only worst decision I'd ever made, but now...I'm not so sure.

As the Jolly Rogers slowly pulls away from port, I watch everything I've ever known slip away from me for the second time. Only this time, it doesn't feel like a punishment worse than death. There's still a twinge of hurt and loss in my chest, but it doesn't feel incapacitating like it did the first time. Still, the consequences of my actions follow me no matter how far we sail away from land.

Needing to keep myself busy and distracted from the plan taking root in my mind, I head below deck. Making a pitstop in my bedroom, I throw on some black leggings and a loose-fitting long-sleeve shirt that hangs off one shoulder. One good thing about not having overly large breasts is that I can go without a bra whenever I choose. I want to be comfortable but also reveal a bit of skin to still feel a little sexy.

After some fussing over my hair, I add some blush, mascara, a thick sweep of eyeliner into a pointed wing, and a light-pink gloss to my lips, then head for the kitchen. My heart rate picks up as I near the doorway, but it falters as I step inside. Instead of Hook, in the kitchen, I find Killian. I try not to let my disappointment show as I approach the island where he's dicing potatoes.

I clear my throat, suddenly nervous about intruding on him and his space. "Hey Killian. I, umm...I could use the distraction if you'd like some help?"

He glances up at me, those dark brown eyes softening as they meet mine and I'm immediately put at ease. I don't know what it is about him. His physical presence alone should be intimidating, and it is, but...something in his eyes tells me I'll never have to be afraid of him. Then again, he's on Hook's ship. Was he headed for Heaven or

Hell before he decided to stay? And if it was Hell, does that automatically make him a bad person? Red was headed to Hell, and I don't think she's a bad person.

"Of course," he says in his deep, rumbling voice, a hint of a smile appearing before he returns his focus to the cutting board. "Would you mind taking over the potatoes?"

I breathe a sigh of relief. "Absolutely! I'd be happy to." Walking to the sink, I wash my hands before taking his place at the island. "So, what's for dinner tonight?"

"Green chile pork stew with Hook's famous jalapeno cornbread."

"I'm not sure I'll ever get used to that," I laugh nervously, still trying to settle my nerves in this new environment.

"Get used to what?"

"Hook being a chef."

"Ahh, yeah, he doesn't really fit the profile with all that leather and jewelry, does he?"

I laugh again, this one coming easier. "Not at all." I picture the beautiful, colorful ink that covers his arms and chest and have to stop myself from biting my lip. "He's quite full of surprises." I let the silence stretch for a bit before I ask the question that's been burning my tongue since I walked in. "I actually thought I'd find him in here cooking. Where is he?"

"Sorry to disappoint."

"What? No!" I put the knife down and look over my shoulder to find him already looking at me, a smirk on his lips and humor in his eyes."

"I'm only teasing. Hook always takes time to talk with each new soul that boards, but he'll be in here soon no doubt. We can't have Hook's famous cornbread without Hook making it now, can we?"

"I suppose not." Returning my attention to the potatoes, I try to keep up the small talk. "So, how did you end up here? In Purgatory?"

Silence stretches and my heart starts to race faster, worried I crossed a line and he's now angry with me. I turn to face him. Everything about his posture tells me he's no longer at ease with our conversation. I can't see more then a small portion of his profile, but he looks...not happy.

"I'm sorry," I rush out. "I'm clearly shit at this small talk stuff. I just thought, well, since I'm stuck here, I may as well try and get to know you, but I understand that your story is just that. *Your story*. And—"

"No, it's fine." He lets out a heavy sigh, his shoulders easing slightly as he turns to face me.

Leaning against the counter, he crosses his arms, which makes me even more aware of how large he is compared to me. How easily he could crush this precious life out of me if he wanted to. But then I meet his eyes again and all thoughts of danger evaporate from my mind. His eyes just look...sad.

"I'm sorry," I start again in a shaky whisper. "I didn't mean to pry."

"If you're going to be a part of this crew, it's only fair that you know our stories and know who we are."

I'm torn between protesting, not wanting to make him relive whatever has his eyes looking so haunted, and desperately wanting to know. Clenching my jaw shut, I lean against the island, hugging myself, and simply nod in agreement. It takes him some time, but he finally finds his voice.

"Growing up, it was always my little sister and I against the world. At least, that's how it felt after our mother died." Before I can ask, he says, "Cancer."

"I'm so sorry, Killian."

"I was eight and my sister was five. We'd always had a picture-perfect family from what I remember, but everything changed after that. My father couldn't handle life without my mother. He started drinking and became a ghost in our home just as much as our mother was. It's like they both died that day." His eyes stare at the floor as he relives his childhood, but I know he's no longer seeing anything in this kitchen. "I did what I could to take care of my sister. I learned quickly how to be the man of the house. At least in the ways I could, making sure she got safely to school and back home every day, getting fed and bathed. We did our best but a few years later my father's ghost materialized. My little sister was growing into a beautiful girl who looked just like our mother. And my father hated her for it."

Oh, God. I hug myself tighter as I prepare myself for the ugliness I know is coming, but I remain still and silent. Listening.

"He started to hit her. I tried to stop him, but I was too little, too weak to fight against a grown man. An angry and hateful drunk. Until I wasn't. I had my growth spurt at sixteen and started hitting the gym hard, joined the football team, learned how to fight back. But by then, it had already been years of abuse. The trauma was already embedded too deep. I vowed to never be anything like him, but my sister wasn't as strong. She ended up marrying a man just like him. Of course, he didn't show his true colors until they were married and had kids of their own. My sister begged me not to do anything. She swore she would leave. But she never did. He always threatened to take the kids away from her and so she stayed."

He pauses, his jaw ticking and muscles bulging as his body tenses with whatever memory is replaying in his head. I want to walk over to him, to put my hand on his arm and tell him that's it ok, but I don't. I stay rooted to my spot, fighting to keep my own emotions from spilling over.

"And she ended up in the hospital with more than just broken bones and bruises. He nearly killed her, and I snapped. I went to their house on a mission. I overpowered him easily, tied him up and got the kids out. I told them to go to the neighbors and stay there. Once they were out of the house, I unleashed all my rage on that motherfucker. I made him suffer in every way he'd ever made my sister suffer. I lost track of how many bones I broke, how many punches I delivered to his face. He was barely alive when I was done beating him, unrecognizable. And when I knew there was no more pain for him left to feel, I slit his throat."

At this admission, his dark eyes finally meet mine again. There's not a hint of regret or remorse to be seen, but he tips his chin in defiance, just like Red did, as if he's preparing for my shocked outrage.

"Apparently, the neighbors decided to call the cops. They came in guns blazing, shooting first. I guess my size and the fact that I was covered in blood, standing over a dead body, was too much for them to handle. I was shot and killed and ended up here because of the guilt I had that I could never protect my sister."

My feet finally move, and I approach him cautiously, though I'm still not afraid of him. He's a protector. I've always felt that about him. I place my hand on his arm and look into his eyes, hoping he can see the sincerity of my words.

"You did protect her. You *died* protecting her. Maybe you couldn't stop the abuse, but you saved her life, Killian. Of that, I'm sure. You did exactly what you needed to."

His eyes slowly soften again, becoming the warm chocolate brown that makes me feel safe. He nods his head and stands up straight. Unlike Red, I don't think Killian wants any more than what I've already offered. No crying. No hugging. So, I let my hand fall from his arm and return to my task of dicing potatoes.

Once the silence becomes comfortable again, I try my hand at actual small talk. "So, how long have you been a part of Hook's crew?"

I smile and relax even more when he answers easily. "About four hundred years, give or take."

"Oh, wow! That's a really long time. So have you been with Hook the longest?"

"No, Smee has, then Sasha, me, Fin, Red, and now you."

"No wonder you guys are such a tight-knit group. That's a long time to be together. Does it ever get old for you?"

I see his large shoulders shrug in my peripheral. "Sometimes. It's the same process over and over again, but the people are always new. The stories are always new. It keeps things interesting enough."

I don't manage to stop my snort before it comes out. "Interesting. Is that what you call orgies?"

I can feel his eyes on me now, the weight of them just as heavy as his body would be. And why am I thinking about the weight of his body? The image of him kneeling behind Red, his wide, muscular frame, large hands practically covering her hips, making her body look impossibly small, flashes through my mind. My cheeks heat and there's no hiding it.

Out of the corner of my eye, I see him move. The next thing I know, his large body is caging me in against the island. He's so wide, but not as tall as Hook. He doesn't have to lean down as far to whisper in my ear. The smell of spices invades my senses as his voice tickles my neck.

"You wanna know what's interesting? You," he admits in a low, sexy voice. "We're all *very* interested to see what you're going to do with us."

My heart is hammering in my chest, not so much as a reaction to Killian, but as a reaction to the situation. Everyone around me is so comfortable with sex, it makes me feel both out of my element and eager to understand why.

Before I can even try to figure out what to do or what to say to Killian, Smee enters the kitchen.

"Oh, princess, you crush me." He dramatically clutches at his heart as he stalks toward me. His words say one thing, but his eyes say something completely different. "That's twice now that you've given Killian something that I want."

Killian is still standing behind me, caging me in, but he hasn't so much as rubbed against me. "I haven't given him *anything*," I say defensively as Smee rounds the island.

Killian removes his right hand from the counter and steps slightly to the side, allowing Smee an opportunity to slide in next to me. I turn to face him which puts Killian at my back and Smee directly in front of me. I'm trapped between them, and I'm totally fucked.

"Maybe not yet you haven't, but you're thinking about it," he says as he reaches for my chin and lifts gently. "I can see it in those big, beautiful eyes and it makes me extremely jealous. But...as you know, I'm not opposed to sharing."

"That will never happen." I narrow my eyes and move to shove him away, but he captures my wrists easily, placing my palms on his stomach and holding them there. I try to jerk my hands free, but I might as well be fighting against steel shackles.

"I know you've seen me, but maybe you need to feel what I have to offer," he smirks as he slowly drags my hands down ridiculously hard abs, forcing them lower and lower.

I try to take a step away from him, but I'm met with an immovable Killian at my back. Despite my verbal rejection, my body has no problem getting on board with whatever is happening. I can't help but react to the attention. Both of these good-looking men have their eyes on *me* and damn if I don't fucking love it. I'm breathing so hard I'm worried I'm about to hyperventilate. And when Smee finally gets my hands to his cock, I think I forget how to breathe entirely.

His smirk turns into a full-blown grin as he rubs my palms up and down the hard length of him. "There it is," he says in a husky voice. "There's that desire I wanted to see. You do want my cock after all. Don't you, princess?"

I open my mouth to protest but Killian's fingers find my bare shoulder, gliding along my skin before softly wrapping his large hand around my neck. He gently pulls me back and I feel his arousal push against me. His words are a direct contrast to the hand wrapped around my neck.

"If you want this, just say yes. But if you don't, all you have to do is tell us to stop."

The weight of Killian's hand on my throat feels suffocating even though he's barely holding me. I still have air to speak but all coherent words have evaporated. All I can process is the feel of Smee's hard dick under my hands, his devious green eyes eagerly waiting for the slightest sign I give him to act on everything they're promising, and Killian's large but safe body behind me. It feels like I'm drowning in the sensations and under their attention. It's too much.

Closing my eyes, I try to find my voice. "I—"

"That's enough." Hook's stern voice cuts through the fog.

Killian immediately releases my throat and takes a step away from me, but Smee holds on to my wrists and thrusts his hips forward against my hand again, a challenge in his eyes, before he finally lets me go.

I stagger slightly, reaching for the island to steady myself as my mind and body slowly come under my control again. Jesus Christ. I have no desire to sleep with Killian or Smee, but I can't deny that being under their attention is heady as fuck. Was I really about to give in to that feeling so easily? Shit.

"If you're staying in this kitchen, you're helping cook dinner. If you don't want to do that, then leave." Hook's voice is angrier than I've heard it before as he makes his way around the island.

I can feel his eyes on me, but I can't bring myself to meet them. "I need some air," I say to no one in particular as I duck my head and walk around the opposite side of the island, getting as far away from him and the other two as I can.

I practically run out of the kitchen and up to the deck. Throwing myself against the rail, I close my eyes and take a deep breath of salty air. My body feels pulled tight as a bowstring and hot as a torch.

"Son of a bitch," I curse, as I let my body sag harder against the rail. It only lasts a second before footsteps make me jump and spin around, all the tension immediately returning as a body comes into view.

"There you are."

Chapter 12

Self Sabotage by MYSSIE

The man who boarded earlier walks up to me and it takes a few seconds to get my bearings. I try to summon the feelings I just had in the kitchen but it's no use. I've never been good at faking it. My face always gives me away, but I need to try anyway.

"I saw you earlier," he drawls.

"I saw you, too." Mr. Captain-fucking-obvious over here. I manage not to roll my eyes.

"I know exactly what your smile meant."

"Oh yeah? And what's that?" I ask in what I hope is a seductive voice.

"That you want me to fuck you as much as I want to fuck you."

For fuck's sake. What is it with this ship and everyone wanting to fuck me? Luckily, this is playing out better than even I had planned, so the smile I give him is genuine when I say, "I'm so glad you found me up here."

Not waiting a second longer, he's on me. I gasp at the suddenness of his body against mine and the feel of his hand around my throat. Unlike Killian's gentle hold, his grip promises nothing but pain. I have to act quickly or else this could go very wrong.

Moving my hands to his jeans, I brush my hands over his cock, already hard and straining against the zipper. "That must be painful," I whisper and then lick my lips, drawing his attention to my mouth. "Let me help."

Slowly, I start to sink lower. His grip around my neck tightens but he allows me to continue until I'm kneeling before him. He leans down, putting his godawful face inches in front of mine, still holding my neck while his other hand reaches for me.

"Look at you, so eager to suck my cock." He shoves two fingers into my mouth, and I barely keep from gagging at the unwanted intrusion. Instead, I force myself to suck on his fingers, giving him the image of what I know he wants to see next.

My hands shake slightly as I reach for his belt, sliding the buckle free and then snapping the button open. The sound of the zipper is loud in my ears, and the bile rising up my throat threatens to ruin everything. I swallow it down as I hold his gaze, putting as much effort as I can into looking innocent and eager.

"Can I?" I ask sweetly, as my hands reach for the top of his jeans. "Please?"

He finally releases his hold on my throat and stands up. I have to fight the urge to rub my neck, but I manage to stay focused on what I need to do next. I slowly pull his pants and underwear down his legs until they're just below his knees. His hard dick springs free, inches in front of my face. My initial thought is he's nowhere near the size of Smee, but I push that ridiculous thought out of my head as I reach for his cock.

"You're so big," I lie, as I wrap my hands around him and begin to stroke.

"Mm, fuck yeah. Stroke me harder, baby."

I do as he instructs, and the second he closes his eyes and tilts his head back, I act. Moving as fast as I can, I wrap my arms around his knees and lift with all my might, pushing to my feet.

"What the fuck are you—"

I manage to get his upper body over the railing, but he reaches out a hand and holds on, preventing me from pushing him all the way over.

"You fucking bitch!" he yells.

I lean down and bite his hand as hard as I can. The metallic taste of blood fills my mouth and a second later he let's go. Gravity does the rest as I tip his legs up higher. One second, he was there, barely holding on. The next, his shout is abruptly cut off when he falls into the ocean.

Leaning over the rail, I check to make sure he isn't holding on to something, about to climb back up and kill me. I can't see him anywhere and the moonlight does nothing to show the water far below us. The sound of my panicked breath is all I can hear as I frantically pat down my body, already knowing I'm not going to find what I need.

"Shit." I slide my hands through my hair and groan.

"Here." Hook's voice startles me, and I scream. He's holding out a small, unsheathed knife to me.

I stare at him for what feels like eternity, waiting for him to take that knife and slam it right through my traitorous heart, but all he does is stand there, holding the knife out to me, hilt first. I finally take it, my hands shaking so bad it's hard to cut, but I finally manage to slice across a finger. Holding it out over the rail, I let my blood drop into the ocean.

Once that's done, all the energy and adrenaline rush out of my body, and I slowly sink to the deck. Leaning my head against the rail siding, I close my eyes and sigh.

"It's done."

I feel Hook lower his large body and sit beside me. So much has happened in the span of ten minutes, Hook catching me at every turn, and I don't want to face him. How much of what just happened did he actually see? I don't want to even imagine the disappointed look in his eyes.

"Your deal with Serene." He says it like a statement, not a

question.

"Yes," I whisper.

"So, is this your plan? Pretend to seduce men and send them to their deaths?"

"I was hoping you didn't see all that."

"I see everything that happens on this ship."

"You might mean that to be comforting, but I assure you, it's not."

"So, is this the plan?" he repeats. "You're just going to throw all my transports overboard?"

"Only the ones that deserve it," I admit, my eyes still closed, my heartbeat finally settling to a normal pace.

"And how did you know he deserved it?"

Letting out a heavy sigh, I finally open my eyes and meet Hook's expectant stare. "I saw it in his eyes the second he looked at me. He would have raped me if I had said no. In fact, he may have liked the fight even more. He was headed to Hell, wasn't he?"

"Just because someone is headed to Hell, doesn't mean they deserve the Nothingness."

"Well, he *did*," I say confidently.

Hook finally nods. "He did."

I sigh again, letting all the tension slip away, leaving me feeling suddenly exhausted. As if he can tell exactly how I feel, Hook's ever-knowing eyes meet mine.

"Taking a soul is a heavy burden to bear."

"He deserved it," I repeat. Even though I know with every fiber of my being that he did, it doesn't make the ache I feel in my chest any lighter. "I don't have a choice," I say, barely above a whisper.

"I know, and that's why I'm going to help you."

My eyes flash to his, wide with the shock I feel at hearing his words. "What?"

"I'm going to help you, but no one else can know. I can't be the one to take a soul, but I'll make sure you don't get hurt. And only the ones who truly deserve it. Do you hear me? If we go months without transporting someone who truly deserves it, then so be it. Only those that deserve it," he insists.

I nod slowly. "Ok. Yes. Only those who deserve it. The worst of the worst."

We sit in silence for several minutes. The only sound is the waves gently crashing against the ship far below. Moonlight shifts on the deck as clouds move in front of it. Despite everything that just happened, I feel a sort of calm settle over me, and I begin to hum. Lyrics start to flow, and before I know it, I'm singing a strange, yet somehow familiar, song.

They say love should be calm and comforting

A warm embrace to keep you safe from the storm

But I want a love that completely consumes

As deep and as dangerous as the sea

With the power to completely destroy me

"Your voice is beautiful, Tink. I was wondering if I'd ever get to hear you sing."

My eyebrows pinch together as I look up at him. "What do you mean?"

He shrugs. "I just figured that's what the tattoo meant."

I'm more confused than ever. "What tattoo?"

He reaches for my arm and turns it around, his thumb gently

rubbing the inside of my wrist. "This one."

As if by magic, like Hook's touch manifested it, I watch as a delicate tattoo appears. A microphone and a music note. My breath catches in my chest as a vivid memory flashes in my mind. The sound of a tattoo gun, the sting of the needles penetrating my skin, and the huge smile on my face as I celebrated getting signed by a record label.

"Tink." Hook's voice sounds concerned as his hand finds my cheek, gently cradling it. "You ok?"

"Yeah…I…." Blinking, the memory fades and Hook's worried eyes come into focus. "I think I just had a memory of my life. I think I was a…a singer."

"Yeah," he echoes. "I think you were."

The revelation is astounding. I sit with the knowledge, letting it sink in, letting it fill me up, a puzzle piece sliding into place. "Holy shit," I whisper in awe as the elation builds. A laugh starts to build in my chest, and I throw my head back and revel in it. "I'm a singer!" I shout to the sky.

Hook's deep laugh pulls my attention back to him. He has the biggest smile plastered on his face, one that I'm sure mirrors my own. His eyes rake over my face slowly, as if he's trying to memorize my features.

"What?" I laugh nervously, wiping at my face. "Do I have something on my face?"

"Happy looks good on you."

Suddenly, I can't meet his intense stare and drop my gaze. "Oh shit, my finger. It's still bleeding." I gesture to my left hand, still resting in his light grip.

"Allow me."

Before I even know what's happening, my pointer finger is in Hook's mouth. His tongue massages the pad of my finger in slow circles before he swirls his tongue around the tip. The very indecent image of him between my legs, swirling his tongue over my clit, makes me moan. I can't even try to hide it. He gently sucks on my finger as he pulls it out of his mouth, making my lips part, my eyes glued to his lips as my finger slides free. He licks his lips and I have to fight not to fall forward and taste them.

"There. All healed."

I look down at my finger and there's no trace of a cut ever happening. "How?"

"Angel, remember?" he says with a cocky grin. This is the Hook I know.

I scoff. "Like you'd ever let me forget."

He pushes to his feet and then offers his hand. Sliding mine into his, I let him easily haul me to my feet. Only, he doesn't immediately let me go. He pulls me flush against his body, but I'm not exactly fighting to get away.

He grabs my chin and forces my head back. God, he's so incredibly tall. My eyes travel up his massive chest, slowing once again on his lips, before meeting serious eyes. "You're going to need to decide soon."

"What?"

"The kitchen," he clarifies. "They're not going to stop until you decide. Either yes or no, Tink. They need to hear you say it. They need rules, clear boundaries, or else they'll continue crossing them. Especially Smee."

"I don't...it's just that...," I sigh. "I'm really confused."

"Well, figure it out soon." Taking a step back, he leans down. Still holding my chin, his thumb traces my bottom lip gently, coaxing the fire inside of me with that one simple touch. His eyes have gone from serious to heated as he lowers his head further. His lips are a breath away from mine, his next words hot on my lips. "I meant what I said in the tub. All you have to do is say yes, little viper. One. Simple.

Word." His warm tongue swipes along my bottom lip and I gasp.

Moving to grab ahold of his shirt, whether to steady myself or pull him closer I'm not sure, I realize I'm still clutching the knife in my hand. I fall back on my heels. *When the fuck did I ever tiptoe?*

My skin is hot, and I know I'm blushing again. Clearing my throat, I hold the knife out to him. "Here. I never said thank you, but…thank you."

He shakes his head. "Keep it. And the next time Smee puts his hands on you, use it."

He turns to walk away, and I can't tell if he's joking or not. "Are you jealous?" I tease, as he continues walking away.

"I'm an angel. I don't get jealous."

"Technically, my hands were on him," I clarify. He doesn't so much as slow down much less stop or acknowledge what I've said.

I guess he really doesn't get jealous.

My fingertip gingerly presses against my lip where he licked me. Pulling my lip into my mouth, I taste a hint of rum and it makes me thirsty. Only, not for a drink. For him.

Shaking my head, I glance down, eyes moving from the knife to my healed finger, to the tattoo now clear as day on my wrist. This can only mean one thing. I'm on the right path.

I'm starting to remember.

Chapter 13

GODDESS by Written By Wolves

Another successful trip to The Gates, but if I'm being honest, I was barely able to focus. I'm starting to see Tink in a whole new light. And I'm not talking about the moonlight, the way it made her skin glow, and how I wanted to undress her slowly, taking in every beautiful inch as it was revealed. The way the breeze blew through her hair and the way her eyes sparkled up at me with so much hope and happiness. And don't even get me started on the smile. The smile that sucker-punched me in my gut. I wanted to smother that brilliant smile only so I could taste it.

Tink isn't who I thought she was. Hell, I don't think she even knew there was more to her than death stares and bitchy remarks. I hardly recognize her as the woman that boarded the Jolly Roger a mere four days ago. I give most of that credit to Red though. That little ball of energy can break anyone down. It's impossible not to love her and her genuine heart. Apparently, Tink is no exception to her charm either.

The sunset I'm currently watching should have all of my attention, but it doesn't. My body may be here, above the clouds, but my mind is still on deck with Tink. I've avoided her for the most part today, trying to give her space to figure out what she wants, but that doesn't mean I don't *see* her wherever she goes. She was on deck most of the day, in another sports bra and tiny pair of shorts, washing the deck. It's a damn good thing I don't need to steer us so much as keep us in a straight line because my attention was on her more than the sea.

The way her tight body moves with each push and pull of the broom. The sheen of sweat glistening on her skin under the golden glow of the sun. Her beautiful voice carrying on the breeze. It hypnotizes me. She hasn't stopped singing since she uncovered that piece of herself and I'm not the only one who seems completely taken by her. The crew does, too. No one has even slightly complained about her being here or her singing. It's like the crew is whole. As if she's always been meant to be here. Our missing piece.

I don't remember turning around, but apparently, I'm done flying as the ship comes into view. Déjà vu runs through me as I see that familiar spot of green on deck. Only this time, as I get closer to landing, she doesn't run away.

Slowing my descent, I flare my wings wide and glide down, easily striding onto the deck without missing a beat. Even if I wasn't looking directly at her, I'd feel her eyes on me. She's not even trying to hide the fact that she's staring, taking in the sight of my wings. Instead of spiriting them away, I keep them out, tucking them in behind me.

"You act like you've never seen wings when I know you've seen Peter's," I point out as I stalk toward her.

"I've only seen his wings a handful of times and yours are so much more…."

"Bigger?" I tease with a cocky grin.

"Captivating," she says in awe, eyes on my wings as I stop directly in front of her. "They're like swirls of light. Like the rays you see falling from the sky through the clouds. Almost as if you could reach out and touch them and feel them slide between your fingers. Can I?" She finally meets my gaze. "Touch them?"

In the blink of an eye, they're gone. "No."

"Oh, of course." Her face falls. I see the embarrassment rising up her cheeks and reach out, lifting her face back up to meet mine.

"Touching an angel's wings is the most intimate thing you can do," I explain. "It's almost like touching our souls. So don't take it personally, but you and I are not at that level."

"I understand," she says quietly, still not wanting to meet my eyes.

"Tinkerbell, look at me."

She slowly raises wide, uncertain hazel eyes up to me, the green around the edges brighter than normal, overshadowing the honey-brown.

"Just because my wings are off-limits doesn't mean the rest of me is." I let go of her chin to lift both of her hands, placing her palms on my chest. "You can touch me anywhere else you'd like. All you have to do is decide. Do you want this? Or do you want what the crew is offering? It's one or the other and they are two *very* different choices. You know what I need to hear from you. All you have to do is say that one simple word."

"You don't sleep with the crew." Not a question. Someone must have already told her.

"No."

I don't know why I'm offering this choice to her. Hell, what am I even offering? Like she said, I don't sleep with the crew. Isn't she now a part of the crew? I should hold her to the same standard, keeping my hands off, but I can't seem to separate my thoughts of her like I do them. There's no denying the chemistry between us, but that's all it is, purely physical. I just keep telling myself that she'll be like any other woman I've slept with. I'll scratch the itch and move on.

Her throat bobs, I can feel the tremble in her hands as I push harder against them, coming in closer. I trail a finger across the swell of her breasts, her chest rising and falling heavily, gliding up the line of her throat where I lift her chin up again, angling her mouth toward mine as I dip lower.

When I'm a mere breath away, I ask, "Do you want the crew?" She shakes her head. "Do you want this?" I feel the slight nod of her head. "The word, Tinkerbell. I need to hear you say it."

"Yes," she breathes against my lips.

My mouth lands on hers. Lips as soft as fucking velvet meet mine and I'm momentarily stunned, overwhelmed by the fluttering in my chest, as if my wings have unfurled inside of me. Then, her lips part and I take the invitation without hesitation, slipping my tongue inside. Hers meets mine in a slow, tentative brush. I can feel the uncertainty in her kiss, understanding that I need to be the one controlling this. I angle her face slightly and take the kiss deeper. I intend to keep it slow and exploratory, but when she moans into my mouth, it's like the trance breaks. In a second, I have her ass in my hands, lifting her to sit on the rail. Her legs wrap around me at the same time her hands wind around my neck, keeping me locked against her.

Our kiss becomes almost frantic. Hungry. As if this is the first and last time either one of us will get this chance. Her hands slide into my hair and squeeze, pulling me harder against her. My hands tighten on her hips where I hold her steady to keep her from falling. When she bites down on my lower lip, a half groan, half growl rumbles in my chest and I have to fight the urge to rip her clothes off.

No.

If we're doing this, we're doing this my way.

Reluctantly, I pull away, breaking our heated kiss, both of us panting and breathless.

"I'm sorry. Did I hurt you?" she asks nervously.

I can't help but chuckle at the thought of this five-foot nothing woman hurting me. "You may be a vicious little viper when you wanna be, but even then, you could never hurt me."

This earns me a scowl, which I fucking love, but it fades quickly as confusion takes its place. "Then, what happened? I thought you wanted to do this."

"If you couldn't tell, I'm very much into this." I glance down and she follows my line of sight.

"Oh...."

Her eyes go wide and her throat bobs again at the outline of my hard cock pushing almost painfully against my leather pants. I ignore the ache in my cock as much as I can, knowing that it will be satiated soon.

"But this isn't how I want this to happen." Grabbing her by the waist, I gently lift her off the railing and set her back down. "Meet back up here when the moon is at its peak," I demand, before turning to walk away.

"What the hell does that even mean?" she shouts after me.

"Midnight, little viper. And come prepared to show those fangs."

"And what the fuck does *that* mean?" I hear her ask, but I'm already making my way below deck.

Luckily, the crew are all gathered in the kitchen. I have to adjust my still hard cock before I step inside. Dinner seems to be well underway by Killian and Red, but I don't pay attention to what they're cooking.

"Listen up," I announce as I storm in. "I need you all on deck at midnight. Do not be late."

Before anyone can ask me a question or even tell me to go fuck myself, which they wouldn't do anyway, I'm already out of sight and storming down the hallway to my bedroom. I have a few hours to kill before midnight and I'm going to need all the time I can get.

Unzipping my pants, I pull my still hard and aching dick out and start stroking. Pent up desire over these last four days has me so worked up I feel close to cumming already. I'm going to have to relieve myself at least three times before I take her, and even then, I hope she's up for an all-nighter because I'm not going to stop fucking her until she's physically unable to stay awake a second longer. I'm going to scratch the fuck out of this itch and be done with it.

I'm not sure how it's possible but the time seems to drag and fly by at the same time. Ten minutes before midnight, my boots make heavy steps across deck in the stillness. Still docked at The Gates, there's no wind or water crashing against the boat to distract me. My leather pants suddenly feel too tight and restricting, and even though my button-down white shirt is opened half-way, I still feel too damn hot. Climbing the six steps up to the platform where the wheel is, I take a seat at the top and wait.

The crew arrive shortly after me, their intoxicated voices preceding their stumbling steps. I didn't demand their sobriety because I'm hoping their slightly incapacitated state will aid the situation.

"The moment you have been waiting for!" Smee announces as he crosses the deck. "Smee is here!" He stops in front of the steps and takes a bow.

His arrogance would annoy me if I knew it wasn't all in good fun. He's actually quite deep and thoughtful but he'd rather die his final death than let most people know that.

"Why are we here, Hook?" Sasha asks with a knowing glint already in her eye. I swear, sometimes she knows me better than I know myself. Then again, she wouldn't have been a very good Black Widow if she wasn't as observant, intelligent, and calculating.

"You'll see in just a moment. Stand off to the side."

Tink emerges from below deck as the crew shuffles off to the side. Her steps falter as she sees them gathered next to me. Even in the moonlight, she can't hide the blush that settles on her cheeks. To her credit, she tips her chin up and keeps walking. I pray desperately that I haven't gauged her incorrectly. I don't pretend to *know* her, but what I've seen and what I've observed, plus what Sasha has also observed, has me confident in my decision.

She stops a few feet away from the steps, where I sit, and glances nervously between me and the waiting crew. She's barefoot and wearing a black silk negligee that hits mid-thigh, a slit lined with green lace clear up to her hip, and green lace covering her breasts giving a wonderful peek-a-boo effect. I want to be able to see every inch of her body, see exactly what color her nipples are, and I'm hoping the sparse moonlight gives her more courage and confidence.

"Oh, this is going to be fun," Red giggles.

"It's only going to be fun if I get to fuck her sassy little mouth," Smee fires back.

"Put a cork in it, Smee," Sasha snaps.

Tinkerbell looks from them and back to me, confusion written all over her face. But underneath that, I see the smallest amount of hurt in her eyes. She thinks I'm giving her to the crew.

"I don't know what's going on or what you think is going to happen but it's *not* happening," Tink declares and turns on her heel.

"Wait!" I bark out the order, no room for disobedience in my tone. She stops and turns but doesn't walk closer. I speak loudly enough for everyone to hear.

"There are rules for tonight." This gets me some grumbling from Smee. I move my gaze from Tinkerbell to the crew. "Hands strictly to yourselves. You can touch yourself but not each other. I want no other distractions happening over here. I want you paying attention, do you understand?" It's clear they're still confused but they all nod. I return my gaze to Tinkerbell, who's standing as still as a statue, anger written all over her face.

"We both know how much you enjoy watching the crew fuck," I state plainly. Snickers erupt from the crew, but I ignore them. "And they love to put on a show, but I think you like the getting attention just as much as you like giving it. So, you and I are going to put on a show, little viper. Now, come here," I demand with a pat to my thigh.

The anger slowly dissipates as my words sink in and she understands what I want. Again, a blush graces her cheeks, and she swallows hard. She's either seconds away from bolting below deck or giving in to her own desire and curiosity and closing the distance between us. I'm watching her face so intently I see the moment she concedes. The moment that's going to change everything. My cock twitches in response as she slowly takes a step towards me.

I shake my head. "No. We're putting on a show, little viper. I want their eyes glued to you. I want them all jealous of what I get to claim as mine. I told you to come prepared to show those fangs." I wait just a few seconds before making my demand. "Crawl to me."

She glances once more at the crew and then back to me. Her hands shake slightly but she reaches down and grabs the end of the negligee, slowly sliding it up her body. I may have said that I want their eyes glued to her but it's mine that are, eagerly soaking up every inch of beautiful skin that's revealed. The swell of her hips, the small, tight waist, the round and perky full breasts, all glowing in the moonlight. She pulls the material over her head and tosses it toward Smee.

He catches it with a devious smile. "Well, well, look who's ready to play," he says as he brings her negligee to his face and inhales her scent.

I only have a second to register the insane possessiveness that comes over me before my eyes are pulled back to Tinkerbell. She slowly lowers her body until her knees hit the deck. Leaning forward onto her hands, her back arches in the most devastating way, and then….

She crawls to me.

She puts all the lethal grace of a panther into her crawl, showcasing all her sun-kissed skin and muscle. Her body moves effortlessly and confidently across the deck. But it's her eyes that capture me and freeze me to the spot. They're locked on mine, and even in the dim light of the moon, I see the power radiating through them.

All her blushes and insecurities are gone. Despite the fact that she's on her hands and knees, she's making her way to me like a fucking goddess walking down a red carpet, demanding the attention of everyone around her. And she has it.

The crew fades away as I watch her climb the steps slowly. Deliberately. Sparkling hazel eyes are all I see as she reaches me, hands resting on my thighs as she kneels between my legs one step below me.

My cock twitches again, reminding me how fucking hard I am as my eyes slowly rake down her body. Fuck, she's beautiful.

"Is this what you wanted?" Her voice is low and seductive, sliding over my skin like the silk negligee she discarded. "To put me in my place in front of the crew?"

I force my eyes up to meet hers. The defiance is clear as day. She may have chosen to do this, but I still see that underlying hurt. This isn't what she expected.

Holding her gaze and patting my thighs, I order, "Sit."

Her chin tips up. I can see her determination not to be shamed or embarrassed as she slowly climbs to her feet and then straddles me. I relish the feel of her in my lap, the heat from her body sinking into mine. Finally, I touch her, sliding my hands across her smooth legs, over the curve of her ass, and then onto her back.

Wrapping my arms around her, I stand, stepping down a few steps before I turn, earning a small gasp of surprise from her. Her legs and arms cling to me. The feeling of holding her in my arms while she holds on to me sets something vicious and primal lose inside me.

I want her to need me.

I want her to want me.

As I gently set her ass down on the landing, her legs fall away from my body, and I lean over her to whisper in her ear.

"Having you crawl to me wasn't about degrading you. It was about empowering you." I pull on her earlobe gently with my lips. "There's so much power in confidence and owning your sexuality. It was about showing you off. Showing off what *I* get to have." I kiss the delicate and sensitive spot just below her ear, feeling goosebumps as I trail my lips down her neck before lifting them to her jaw. "It was about every pair of eyes on you, wanting you, imagining you crawling to *them*." My next words are whispered against her lips. "It was about leveling the playing field. Because I didn't want to be the only one on my knees."

When I pull back, her eyes are wide in shock, her breathing already ragged, betraying her feigned bravado. I don't want her faking it. I want her confident beyond all measure. I want her to demand the attention she deserves, and I want her to thrive in it.

Slowly lowering my body, I kneel two steps below her. Holding her gaze, my fingertips find her ankles and glide slowly up her smooth legs, feeling the arc of her calves before stopping on the inside of her knees. I make it extremely clear what I'm about to do, giving her the opportunity to stop this if this is going too far. She doesn't say a word and her eyes haven't left mine, not even for a second. If the crew being here watching is bothering her, she hasn't let it show.

Pushing her legs open, I finally break our gaze. She's spread-out before me and my cock aches against my pants as I take in every inch of her naked body. Even in the moonlight, I can see her beautiful pussy glistening, already wet just from the attention and the promise of what's to come.

Reaching out, I slide a finger up the middle of her pussy. She sucks in a shaky breath, closing her eyes for a second before finding mine again.

"Look who likes being watched." I smirk. "Already so damn wet."

The memory of her taste on my tongue has me lowering my head, desperate for another hit. I wanted to draw this out, take my time and explore every inch of her, get her so frenzied that she begs me for more. But just like the kiss earlier, I can't seem to stop myself. Pushing her thighs wider, I slide my tongue up the center of her pussy, parting her lips and finally tasting her again. She lets out a low groan, body shivering underneath me. I close my eyes as I make another pass, greedily licking up everything she has to offer.

When my tongue caresses her clit, she sighs, and a soft, "Fuck," slips from her lips as her body finally starts to relax. She falls back to rest on her forearms, but her eyes stay glued to what I'm doing. I want to hear her beautiful voice moan and cry out with pleasure more than I've wanted anything in a long time. Even though my insides feel frenetic, I manage to control my movements, kissing her pussy deliberately.

Keeping my tongue and mouth focused on her clit, I use my fingers to tease her opening, barely sinking in the tips of my fingers.

"Holy shit, that feels good," she says in a beautiful, airy voice, followed by a long, drawn-out moan.

Rolling my eyes up, I catch the moment her eyes flutter closed, and she lies all the way down, submitting to the pleasure.

"Oh, God, yes!" Her back arches when I finally slide my fingers all the way inside, moving them in and out slowly as I continue to lick and suck her clit.

Her body is moving now, hips slightly rocking up and down against my tongue. Her breath is coming in pants in between moans and whimpers that have my chest tightening and cock aching. But when her hands sink into my hair and my name graces her pleasure-filled lips, my control breaks.

I growl into her, my strokes becoming harder and faster as my fingers pump inside her.

"Fuck, right there. Don't stop, Hook. Please don't stop," she begs, tugging on my hair.

Her scent.

Her taste.

Her warmth.

My name on her lips.

Feeling the same need to be closer, I wrap my free arm around her leg and pull her further off the edge, holding her mercilessly against my mouth as I keep fingering her and sucking her.

"Oh, my god, you're going to make me cum." Her voice is squeezed tight, and I can feel her body coiling and tightening.

I keep my pace steady, never once wavering as her body begins to rock faster. She's seconds away from breaking apart in my hands and I moan my own pleasure into her as the orgasm hits. When she cums, her body sings just as beautifully as she does.

Legs shaking.

Stomach spasming.

Back arching.

Hands gripping.

Voice screaming.

Her pussy squeezes and releases my fingers, soaking them with her cum as I suck her clit into my mouth, drawing out her orgasm. When her body stops jerking and her hands finally release their death grip on my hair, I slide my fingers out of her. Giving her one final lick from bottom to top, drinking down her juices, I reluctantly pull away.

Her body is completely limp as she lies on the platform, but her eyes are full of life as they meet mine. The way she's looking at me, drinking me in, lights a fire in my gut so hot it feels like I'll burst into flames. My cock is so fucking hard it actually hurts. I need a release like I need air to breathe.

"I need to be inside you. Right. Fucking. Now," I growl like a beast as I lean down and scoop her into my arms.

She grabs ahold of me and hangs on as I step onto the platform and place her on the rail, just like I did earlier. With one hand holding her, I manage to unzip my pants and free my cock with the other. I don't allow her any time to second-guess or protest as I line my cock up to her opening and push inside.

"Hook." My name is a gasp on her lips as the head of my cock sinks in.

"Goddammit," I say through clenched teeth as I push in deeper. "So fucking tight and wet."

I fight for every inch, reveling in the feel of my cock spreading her wide, making room for me until I'm finally able to glide in and out. She feels so fucking small in my arms, it feels like I could actually break her if I fuck her like I want to. So, instead, I hold back, giving her long, slow strokes that only add to the fire burning inside me.

"God, you're so deep." Her voice is a mere whisper against my neck as she clings to me. "You feel impossibly good," she admits.

I don't know if she meant to say it out loud, but I'm glad that she did because I feel the exact same way.

She feels too good to be real.

When I pull out and give her shallow strokes, her voice hitches and she throws her head back. "Yeah, just like that," she pants. "Fuck, you're going to make me cum again. Don't stop."

Feeling her cum on my fingers is one thing, but feeling her pussy clench around my dick is almost too much to take. When she opens her mouth to scream into the night sky, I grip her chin and pull her head down, claiming her mouth with my own. Swallowing down her voice, her moans, her breath, I hope and pray that it puts out this wildfire burning furiously and uncontrollably through my body and fucking soul.

It only adds fuel to the flames.

I break the kiss only to draw air into my lungs. We're both breathing hard, gasping for air between moans and curses. Her hands are in my hair again and mine are gripping her hips, fingers digging into her soft, delicate skin. I have a second to consider the fact that I might be hurting her but that thought rushes away as my orgasm rises out of nowhere.

"I'm gonna cum." The words fall out of my mouth in a rush. I hold on tighter as I slam into her, barely holding back. She cries out as I hit deep, again and again and again, my own moans adding a lyrical melody to her song. I push in one last time, holding on to her as my cock pulses and spills inside her.

"Fuuuck," I groan as the orgasm rips through me. My legs shake and my entire body shudders with the force of it. I've never cum this fucking hard in my life.

As the orgasm fades, I loosen my grip on her and let my head fall to her shoulder. The only sounds are our heavy breaths and the loud thud of my heart hammering against my ribs. But then comes the applause.

The world seems to snap back into place around me and I suddenly remember the crew that's standing a few feet away. This was all for show, except I completely forgot I was performing. Lifting my head off Tink's shoulder, I briefly meet her gaze, a blush already burning her cheeks.

I slide out of her and tuck myself back in my pants before sliding my arm under her knees and lifting her up, holding her against my chest. Walking down the steps, I barely acknowledge the crew as we walk by.

"We're done here," I tell them. As I make my way to the stairs that lead below deck, I meet Tink's gaze. "Except you. I'm not nearly done with you yet."

Her eyes go wide, and she swallows hard, but she nods her head in agreement. Fuck. A part of me is screaming to take her to her bedroom and be done with it, let her join the crew, but the itch isn't even close to being scratched. A small voice warns me that it never will be, but I ignore it as I take her to my bedroom.

Just one night.

Fuck her until I can't fuck her anymore. It's always been enough before. This isn't any different. And as I kick the door closed behind us and lay her down on my bed, I shut out all other thoughts. My only focus for the next few hours is pleasure. This will end when the moon falls from the sky.

When the sun rises on a new day, this night and...*this* will be over.

Chapter 14

Beep.

      Beep.

            Beep.

The familiar sound from my dream rouses me from a deep sleep. Honestly, the best sleep I've had in a long time. Blinking my eyes, it takes a few seconds to adjust to the brightness. It's clearly way past dawn and I'm still in bed. The slight sway of the ship tells me we've already left port. No one has come to force me out of bed or to even check on me.

My bedroom.

I'm in *my* bedroom.

I don't remember coming back here. The last thing I remember is seeing stars. Not stars in the night sky but stars from a mind-blowing orgasm. And then Hook's face above me, his sweaty hair clinging to his temples and his eyes just as lost to the stars as I imagine mine were.

Was last night just a dream?

As I push myself into a sitting position, the ache between my legs reveals that it was absolutely *not* a dream. The rest of the night comes flooding back. Me, on deck, crawling to Hook, naked…*in front of the crew!* I can still smell him on me. The scent of sex and salty sea-air.

"Oh, God," I grumble, rubbing my hands down my face.

I wonder how long I can hide out in my room before I have to actually face them. And Hook? I don't even want to know what the vibe between us is going to be like now. After a night of fucking each other's brains out, I woke up in my bed. Alone. If that's not a huge statement about what last night was then I don't know what is. Hook clearly only wanted to make a show of claiming me but doesn't want me enough to wake up to me in the morning.

He made it very clear that he only wanted to have me once before the crew got to have me. Last night was nothing more than proving a point. He's the captain, and he gets whatever he wants. I'm not surprised. Not really. So why the fuck does it feel like I just got hit with a baseball bat to the chest?

I thought being forced to leave Sinful Delights was painful, but this...this is so much worse. At least Sinn never pretended to like me, much less want me. I thought it was brutal to go unseen, to feel so alone for so long, but this....

To feel truly seen. To feel wanted and desired, only to be used and then discarded. I thought Hook was the better brother because he's nicer, more open, and he seems to actually care about his crew and the souls he ferries, but I was wrong. Sinn never tried to hide his cruelty, so you could never really be hurt by his actions.

Hook's cruelty is much more treacherous.

He fooled me. And I fucking fell for it.

Anger and embarrassment rush through me in equal measure. I'm pissed at myself for taking his words and making them seem like more than what they were. I mean, the things he said, the way he kissed me. Hell, even helping me with my deal with Serene. He doesn't have to do that. I was hoping that maybe he saw something in me like I see in him. Something special. I was hoping that maybe he felt the same pull to me that I do to him. It's clear now, in the bright light of day, that my hope was foolish.

As much as I want to stay in this room and hide away, I'm not a fucking coward. I'm stuck on this ship for the foreseeable future, I can't let this define me. Besides, people can only make you feel a certain way if you let them, right? Well, fuck Hook, fuck Sinn, and fuck everyone else too. I'm not going to let what happened last night get to me. I had amazing sex. I got mine and he got his. There's nothing to be ashamed about. No one has to know any more than that. What I'm feeling inside doesn't need to be announced. No one will know but me.

Tossing the covers off, I walk to the dresser. The negligee I wore last night is folded on top. Slipping it back on, I rummage through the drawers, pulling out a pair of light-blue cut-offs and a white tank top, then grab my laundry basket and head out.

First, laundry.

Second, shower and get the smell of Hook off me.

Luckily, I don't run into anyone while I'm up and about. With my laundry in the dryer, I debate what to do next. A small part of me wants to be the coward and lock myself away in my room, but I don't want anyone to have anything to use against me. Plus, I feel better now that I'm clean and smelling like myself again. No one has to know how I feel about what happened last night or how I felt waking up. I can play the game of easy nonchalance.

Walking into the lounge, my eyes dart from one end to the other, taking in the space and trying to figure out what I'm going to do with my time. Should I be up on deck helping the crew? Probably. But fuck that. Fuck what Hook wants. If they wanted me up there, they would have come to get me. I'm not going to volunteer my free labor. Is it wrong to leave the crew hanging? Yes. But it's not like I'm *actually* helping anyway.

Spotting a bookshelf, I walk over to it and browse the titles, looking for horror or thriller, something stabby to suit my mood. Finding one that looks promising, I slide it out and read the blurb and reviews.

"Heart-pounding page turner that you can't put down."

"Bloody. This one isn't for the faint of heart."

"A twist that will leave you shook."

Honestly, they sold me at bloody. I debate pouring a glass of wine from the kitchen but decide against it. I should definitely keep a clear head. Alcohol will only heighten my emotions and I don't want to lose control. Not until I've put last night behind me. So, I lie down on one of the couches and throw my legs up over the back of it and crack open my book.

"There you are!" Red's cheery voice pulls my attention away from the pages.

"We were wondering where you've been hiding," Smee adds with a teasing smirk as he follows behind Red.

I roll my eyes and gesture to where I'm lying on the couch in the very open and public lounge. "Clearly not hiding."

Red throws herself down on the couch and grabs my legs, placing them in her lap as she turns to me excitedly. "Tell me everything!" she squeals.

"Maybe not everything," Smee adds as he lifts my shoulders up and scooches in underneath me.

"Hey!" I cry out in protest, but he drapes his arm over my stomach, holding me in place.

"I see you two have found her," Sasha points out as she enters the room with both Fin and Killian on her heels.

I let out an exasperated sigh. "It's not like I was hard to find. I've been right here."

"Have you been in here all day?" Red asks.

Looking down at the book still open in my hands, I notice that I'm already three-quarters of the way through it. Damn, I guess I have been in here all day.

"Yeah, I guess so. This book really pulled me in. I completely lost track of time. What time is it?"

"Playtime." Smee looks down at me and wiggles his eyebrows.

I roll mine again as Red answers. "I'm not sure but it's sundown and dinner is already in the oven, so no need to do anything other than dish about your night last night. Girl! How was it? Was it divine?" she hints to our conversation from the day before.

Closing the book, I grab Smee's arm and lift it off me. He lets me but keeps his arm around my shoulder as I sit up. I'm squished between him and Red while the other three sit on the couch across from us. Everyone's at ease, even Fin, as he leans in resting his shoulder against Sasha's.

And all eyes are on *me*.

I'm suddenly way more nervous sitting here with them now, fully dressed, than I was last night crawling naked in front of them. Just the memory has my cheeks heating.

"Don't be embarrassed." The soft, quiet voice of Fin shocks me. It's the first time I've heard him speak, much less directly to me. He's looking up at me through a mess of curls, but his dark brown eyes are steady and confident. "We know you've seen us, and we're not embarrassed." He shrugs. "What happened last night is normal on this ship."

"Well…," Red interrupts, "Hook sleeping with one of us isn't exactly normal, but the rest, yeah. Totally! And girl, you looked smokin' hot." She fans herself.

"Thanksss, I guess? I mean, this is all normal to you guys, but it's not to me. It's going to take me some time to get used to it."

Smee chuckles. "Don't downplay what you did last night. You

were good and you know it. Imagine how good we would be together."
His fingertips start running up and down my bare arm.

"Stop that." I swat at his fingers. He does but keeps his arm over my shoulder, arrogant smirk in place.

"Well?" Sasha asks, a knowing glint in her eye as she appraises me.

"Well, what?" I ask, acting like I don't know what she's talking about.

"How was it?" she repeats Red's question.

I shrug, trying with all my might to play it off. To not let one ounce of the hurt I felt this morning come rushing back. Instead, I cling to the anger of being used, the anger of being discarded, not by one angel but now by two.

"It was fine. It was sex. He gave me orgasms and I gave him some. You all know how it works. Not much else to tell."

From the look on everyone's faces, no one believes me. For once, I'm thankful it's Smee that comments, taking the heat off me by making the conversation about him.

"If it was me you spent the night with, I guarantee you'd be singing me praises."

"Oh yeah?" I cock an eyebrow as I look at him doubtfully.

"Yeah." He leans over, grabbing my chin and looking at me with so much confidence and heat in his eyes, I can't help but believe him. "Because I'm not an angel, princess. I'm not afraid to fuck you like the sinner I am."

I swallow, feeling desire pool low in my gut, but not because of Smee. Because I remember every sinful thing Hook did to my body last night. Every filthy word he spoke. Every time he took the Lord's name in vain right alongside me. They clearly have no idea who Hook is behind closed doors. But I do. And fuck, I would sell my soul to get another night with him.

But I won't. Because I deserve better than that. So, I let Smee think the desire in my eyes is for him, and I try to connect these feelings with him. It's clear I'm free to fuck whoever I want now, so why not give Smee a chance?

His eyes widen in shock when I move to straddle him, but he recovers quickly, giving me that arrogant smirk. His green eyes flash with a challenge as I rock my hips in his lap, feeling him grow hard underneath me. His hands grip my ass and pull me even harder against him.

"Am I the only one that thinks this is a really bad idea?" I hear Sasha ask the others, but I ignore them, giving all my focus to Smee.

"I knew you'd come around sooner or later. I saw the way you looked at me that first night."

"I've never denied you're beautiful," I admit, tracing his lips with my fingertips.

His smirk turns into a wide grin. "Don't fall in love with me, princess. I'm not a man to be tied down."

"Oh, Smee. What makes you think I only want you?" I tilt my head to the side, waiting for him to answer.

He looks confused and I laugh as I climb off his lap, turning and heading toward Killian. Killian's warm eyes roam over my body before meeting mine as I step closer to him. He doesn't object as I climb onto his lap, straddling him the way I just did Smee. I know that choosing Killian over him will drive him mad. He may tease about being jealous, but I know he's not used to being turned down.

Killian's large hands move to rest on my thighs, not nearly as presumptuous and aggressive as Smee, but just as eager. I can see it in the way he looks at me. Hell, the way they all look at me. This is what they know. This is what they do.

"What about you, Killian?" I ask as I slide my hands up his broad chest. "Will you fuck me like a sinner too?"

I feel his body tense seconds before a large arm wraps around my waist and I'm being hauled off him. Hook's scent slams into me like a car hitting a brick wall. I'm momentarily hypnotized, my body now intimately familiar with his scent, his body, and what it does to me. After my head clears, I begin to struggle in his hold, kicking and squirming, trying to break free.

"Hey! What the fuck is your problem?" I yell incredulously. "Let me go!"

My demands fall on deaf ears, and just like that first day he threw me over his shoulder, it's impossible for me to escape. It doesn't stop me from fighting though. From allowing the anger to rise and happily giving it an outlet. He threw me away like used goods last night and now he has the audacity to rip me off Killian? Why?

He storms up the steps, taking us topside, and the cool night air feels good against my heated skin. Then, Hook's arm releases me so suddenly I fall to my knees on the deck.

"What in the actual fuck, Hook?"

I'm pushing myself to my feet when he grabs ahold of my right arm, jerking me up. Before I realize what's happening, one of the many ropes from the ship's rigging is tied tightly around my wrist.

"What the hell is this?" I demand as I frantically fumble at the knot with my left hand.

That arm is then pulled forcefully and tied to another rope. Hook walks to where the ropes are connected to the mess of rigging and he tightens them, pulling my arms out wide to each side. I'm literally tied up and it happened in a matter of seconds.

"Hook, what the fuck are you doing?" Anger rushes through my veins but so does excitement. I ignore the desire swirling in my gut and yell at him instead. "Answer me!"

The crew emerges from below deck, everyone obviously eager to watch the shit show. I fight against the ropes, causing them to tighten and rub painfully against my skin. I ignore the pain and continue to struggle helplessly.

"Red, help me," I plead. "Untie me."

She shakes her head and takes a step back. Fuck. It looks like the crew isn't going to do anything to come to my aid. They're not going to go against their captain and they're probably just as excited to watch whatever is happening unfold. Fuck them.

"No one is going to help you." Hook finally speaks as he approaches me.

He sets down a bucket a few feet away from me. The moonlight reflects off the water inside. I fight harder against the ropes until Hook steps into my space and I freeze.

"What the fuck are you doing?" I demand again.

"Teaching you a lesson," he says calmly.

I scoff. "A lesson? A lesson for what?"

He leans in, whispering the words so only I hear them. "To learn to keep your hands to yourself." There's a bite in his tone that I don't recognize.

I stop fighting against the ropes as he steps away just far enough to look at me. "Wh…what?" I can barely get the word out.

Once again, his words say one thing while his actions say another. I'm so fucking confused I think I might actually have brain damage from the whiplash.

He ignores my question, letting his eyes slowly trail down my body. My nipples harden under his heated gaze, and I can't hide the shiver that slides up my spine.

His nostrils flare but his voice is back to being calm and even. "White shirt. No bra. You really do love the attention, don't you, little viper?"

"You said you wanted me to be confident and thrive in it." I tip my chin up in defiance.

He reaches down and grabs the bucket of water, throwing it at me. The freezing cold sea water makes me gasp in shock. The air is pulled from my lungs, and it takes a few seconds before I can breathe again. I instantly start shivering for an entirely different reason.

Narrowing my eyes, I seethe, "You fu...cking...bas...tard." The insult doesn't quite land as I stutter through chattering teeth.

"Look at you," he says as he slowly walks in a circle around me. "Tied up and soaking wet. In more ways than one I'd bet."

"Screw you," I hiss.

"That can most definitely be arranged." His warm breath caresses my ear and neck, and his beard tickles my shoulder, sending goosebumps trailing over my cold skin.

His words catch me off guard. Frankly, this entire situation has me fucked up. I don't know what he wants. He walks back in front of me, eyes taking in my breasts, clearly displayed in the wet tank top that's stuck to my freezing skin. My nipples are so hard I'm afraid they might slice through the thin material.

"You look cold," he says matter-of-factly. And then, he leans down, taking a nipple in his mouth.

My body involuntarily arches into his touch. The warmth of his mouth on my cold nipple makes my entire body shudder. I moan as he swirls his tongue around and around before sucking a huge chunk of my breast into his mouth and letting go with a loud pop.

Next thing I know, a knife is in his hand and he's slicing my shirt from top to bottom and then at the shoulders, pulling it off me. I cry out as he slaps one breast and then the other. My cold, numb skin sends little needles of pain through me with each slap.

Then, his hand is around my jaw, jerking my face up as stormy blue eyes lock with mine. "I thought I made it very clear, Tinkerbell," he says in a low, deep whisper. "The crew or me. Not both."

"I...." I swallow. I don't even know what to say. I'm at a

complete loss for words. My mind is still trying to catch up with everything that's happening and everything he's insinuating.

"Was I not enough for you?" he asks, slightly loosening his hold on my jaw. The question is barely more than a whisper. And behind the anger in his eyes, I see something familiar.

Hurt.

"Yes, but you...." I trail off, unsure of how to move forward. His words from the tub have been raging loud in my head all day.

Maybe I'm the selfish captain who wants to have you first. Touch you first. Taste you first. Fuck you first.

First. Insinuating that the crew would have me after he did. Insinuating that all he wanted was to fuck me and be done with me, which is exactly what played out last night. And now he has the nerve to look hurt? As if I'm the one who hurt him and not the other way around?

His eyes dart back and forth between mine, clearly trying to read what I'm thinking, but *I* don't even know what I'm thinking, so I have no idea what he sees.

He lets go of my face to unbutton my shorts, dropping down to drag them down my legs, lifting my feet to remove them, leaving me standing completely naked. Tied up and fucking freezing.

He moves to stand behind me again, pressing his body against mine, showing me that he's already hard. His body heat alone makes me sigh and I close my eyes, focusing on how good he feels pressed up against me. I want to sink into him. I gasp as a quick slap to my cheek pulls me out of my lull.

"Open your eyes and look at them." He grabs my chin again, holding my face forward where the crew stands a few feet away, watching. His right hand slides down my stomach and between my legs. He wastes no time, dipping two fingers inside me, making me moan again.

"Do you see somebody you want standing over there?" he whispers in my ear. "Maybe you want to get a taste of all of them?"

I shake my head.

He moves to rub my clit, no teasing in his touch. I can already feel the orgasm building inside me. One night with me and he knows exactly how to make my body sing. My legs begin to shake, and my arms pull at the ropes, digging them in deeper, but it's a faint pain compared to the wave I feel surging low in my gut.

"Oh, God, you're going to make me cum."

"Maybe you like their hands on you more than mine," he bites out, and removes his hand from between my legs, depriving me of my release.

"No!" I shout, partly to his statement and partly to him leaving me on the edge of an orgasm.

"No what, Tinkerbell?"

"I don't want anyone else, Hook, please," I beg.

"It didn't look like you didn't want anyone else when I literally had to pull you off Killian," he growls in my ear. "They may have fun together, but I. Don't. Share."

"Ok. I didn't know you wanted me more than just last night. I didn't mean…I didn't know."

I hear his zipper slide down and then he's brushing the head of his cock against my slick pussy. His foot kicks my feet, spreading my legs wider. The hand that's still gripping my face pulls my head to the side where I meet his frenzied gaze.

"Mine," he says through clenched teeth as he pushes inside me, hard, ripping a loud cry from my throat.

I close my eyes and try to throw my head back, but he's still holding it hostage.

"Look at me," he demands as he pulls out of me. Opening my eyes, I see the truth of his words written all over his face. "Mine," he repeats as he slams into me again.

His lips crash onto mine in a desperate, messy kiss. Our tongues fight against each other as if to speak all the words neither one of us can say. He bites down on my bottom lip, almost painfully before he releases my face and grabs my hips with both hands. Sagging in the ropes, I lean forward as much as I can as he fucks me from behind, mercilessly. His hard cock slides in and out of me at a pace I didn't even know was possible. It's frantic. It's rough. But I can tell, even in this state, he's holding back.

"Fuck, you feel so good," he pants, gripping my hips even tighter. "Let me feel your tight pussy soak my cock. Cum for me, little viper."

As if I have no choice but to do what he says, my orgasm surges and crashes around us so powerfully it feels like I'm going to splinter apart like a ship against the angry sea. I vaguely hear myself crying out, and Hook's deep voice urging me on before he follows me over the edge.

The only thing keeping me standing are the ropes tied to my wrists. When they finally release me, I'm literally dead weight in Hook's arms. As he carries me below deck, the adrenaline fades and my body starts to ache, not just between my legs but my wrists and all my muscles, as the cold penetrates through my skin and into my bones. My body starts to shake uncontrollably, and I can't stop it.

"Hang on, Tink." Hook's voice rumbles through his chest, softer than he's been all night. "I'll get you warmed up."

Chapter 15

Fix by True North

What the fuck am I doing? I should just carry her ass back to her room and put her in bed, alone, to warm up. Instead, I'm filling up the gigantic jacuzzi tub with warm water and essential oils to help her body relax.

Hell, I shouldn't have even done what I did tonight. I should have just left it for what it was. One night. Like I said I would. But when I walked by the lounge and saw her climb onto Killian's lap, something inside of me snapped. Sure, I felt irritation before when she had been between Killian and Smee in the kitchen, and at seeing Smee try so hard to get her to sleep with him, but this was different.

This was intense possessiveness.

After spending the night completely lost in her, exploring every inch of her body and learning how to make it fucking sing for me, it feels like.... Fuck. It feels like she was made for me. I tried to ignore the voice in my head telling me the truth I didn't want to hear. I tried to keep it to simply fucking. That's why I didn't let her fall asleep in my bed. The last thing I need muddying up my brain any more than it already is, is cuddling and pillow talk.

Or waking up to her soft body pressed against mine. Or slipping under the covers to coax her out of sleep by having breakfast in bed before kissing my way up her body to claim her mouth and slide inside her.

The thoughts alone are maddening.

I needed time alone to clear my head.

I left her alone all day in an effort to distance myself from her and whatever it is I'm fucking feeling. Then I saw her in Killian's lap. I played it off well enough, making it all about the physical aspect and saying nothing of feelings. I held on tightly to the force of possessiveness I felt and let that be my excuse for what I did, but underneath that was something far worse. Something terrifying.

Pain.

The thought of anyone else getting to see Tink the way I did last night felt like a hot poker being stabbed into my chest. Sure, the crew saw what we did on deck but that's different. They *watched* her but they didn't *have* her. They didn't taste her. They didn't feel her. They didn't have those beautiful hazel eyes locked on them like they were the only thing of consequence in the entire universe. And the thought of Tink looking at anyone else the way she looked at me last night....

I'd rather be tied to the anchor and dropped in the sea to drown than see her look that way at someone else. I never even saw her look at Peter the way she looked at me right before she passed out.

I undress as the tub fills and then shut off the water before returning to Tink. She's fallen over on the bench, curled on her side, hugging herself as her body shakes almost violently. Shit. Now I feel like a fucking asshole for throwing the freezing cold sea water on her. Scooping her into my arms, I carry us both into the tub and slowly lower us into the warm water. Even though I didn't make it as hot as it was last time we were here, I know the change in temperature is going to hurt her before it feels better.

She whimpers as the water envelopes us, and I grit my teeth at the sound. Hearing her in pain sends a sharp pain straight to my heart. And her pain is one hundred percent my fault. I mentally kick myself in the ass for letting my anger get the best of me. But damn if seeing her touch another man didn't fucking piss me the fuck off.

After a few minutes, her body stops shaking but she remains tense in my hold. The silence becomes heavy, and I can practically feel her discomfort with our situation like it's as physical as her body.

She lifts her head off my chest. "Thank you. I'm better now." She tries to pull out of my hold, but I grip her tighter. She sighs, closing her eyes for a second before opening them and looking up at me. Her voice sounds tired when she asks, "Hook, what are you doing?"

I know what she's asking but I still can't quite get my brain to accept what my heart seems to already know. So, I give her the only truth I can.

"Taking care of what's mine."

A small, humorless laugh escapes her mouth. "What's yours? I'm not a possession you can own."

She pushes against me, harder this time, and I reluctantly let her go. The water immediately feels colder without her body in my lap. She moves all the way to the other end, sitting across from me and leveling me with one of her shrewd stares. Seeing the old Tink looking back at me is like a slap in the face.

Running my hand down my face, I grumble, "You know what I mean."

"No, Hook, I actually don't." She shakes her head. "Your words say one thing and then your actions say another. Honestly, I don't think a psychic would know what you mean."

Fair. I've been all over the fucking map when it comes to her, but I'm not going to admit that I'm just as fucking confused as she is. So, I stick to what I do know.

"If I didn't make it clear before, I'm positive I made it clear tonight. I don't share."

"So, all this...," she gestures between us, "and all that...," she throws her arm up indicating what happened above deck, "is all about *sex*?"

"What else would it be about?"

She scoffs and shakes her head. "We're clearly not on the same page. Last time we were in this tub, you kept saying the word first. You get to touch me *first*. You get to fuck me *first*. Indicating that the others would get me *second*. And after last night, when I woke up in my bed, *alone*, I figured that was it. You were done with me. And then you have the audacity to—"

"I'm clearly not done with you," I interrupt.

"Clearly," she deadpans. "So...what, Hook? You want to fuck me until you're tired of me?"

My jaw aches at how hard I'm clenching my teeth together. I don't want to lie to her or lead her on, but I can't tell her what she so clearly wants to hear until I know, without a shadow of a doubt, what I want.

"You make it sound like a bad thing. Like I'm using you. No one forced you to sleep with me, Tinkerbell. *You chose*," I say forcefully. "You're getting just as much out of this as I am. Are you not? Did last night not satisfy you?"

"You know it did, but—"

"But what?" I push. "What's so wrong with satisfying our urges together? You can't tell me you don't want more after last night."

She opens her mouth to protest and then closes it.

"The only thing I ask is that you don't fuck the crew. I think that's a pretty easy ask."

"Don't fuck the crew until you're done with me, is that it?"

Fuck, it feels like my teeth are going to crack under the pressure I'm putting on them. The thought of her ever fucking the crew makes me see fucking red, but I don't know what else to say. I can't promise her a happy ever after. The one thing I have in common with my brother is the fact that neither one of us ever gave a thought to commitment. Well, he may have crossed that bridge before I did, but

I'm not certain that bridge even exists for me. I've always planned to go back to Heaven, so anything in this realm, anything with Tinkerbell, would end at some point. Plus, I don't know that what I'm feeling right now isn't just infatuation.

"Take it or leave it." I throw the offer in front of us, giving her the choice, once again, to decide.

"And if I want the freedom to fuck the crew or whoever else I want?"

Suppressing the intense anger that question ignites in me, I answer as calmly as I can, trying to appear nonchalant. "Then fuck whoever you want, and we're done here."

So many emotions seem to flash through her eyes as she contemplates my offer. It feels like she's literally holding my balls in her hand. It's all up to her whether she's going to caress them, or fucking crush them. We stare at each other as the seconds drag on, the tension so thick between us it's almost suffocating.

I start to question whether last night was as good for her as it was for me. I start to question if I saw something in her eyes that wasn't even there at all. Maybe what I saw was just the effects of multiple orgasms and had nothing at all to do with how she was feeling.

"Fine," she finally says. "The same rules apply to you. We fuck each other and no one else."

"Done," I agree quickly, the tension finally leaving my body. As I move to close the distance between us, she holds up a hand, stopping me.

"Don't." It's an order, and there's no room for negotiation in her tone. "After the shit you just pulled, the last thing I want to do is fuck you right now."

She glides through the water, moving to the edge and then climbs out. Water drips down her sexy body and I finally notice some bruising on her hips and legs in the form of fingerprints. My fingerprints.

Then, my eyes slide down her arms to where her wrists are red, skin raw and angry from where the ropes cut into her. Fucking hell. I've already hurt her so much. No wonder she doesn't want to spend another second with me. Hell, looking at her injured body, I'm surprised she said yes to sleeping with me at all.

Clenching my fists, I have to fight the urge to reach for her. To pull her back into the water with me and let her body relax. To kiss every bruise and massage every sore muscle. But that's not the deal we made. Fucking and just fucking. Maybe if I repeat it enough, I'll start to believe it.

Instead, I watch her wrap a towel around herself and leave the bathroom without so much as a glance back at me or a *fuck you, Hook* on her way out.

"Fuck me," I grumble to myself as I sink further into the water, resting my head against the edge and staring up at the ceiling.

What did I just do? A question that seems to be recurring lately. I'm being completely selfish by not letting her go. By dangling the smallest piece of myself out to her knowing damn well it's unfair. But my need to have her overrides my ability to do what's right. Just because I'm an angel, doesn't mean I'm a saint. Clearly, I'm fucking not.

Maybe this is why The Gate home has remained closed to me. Maybe this is why I don't feel the pull to cross over anymore. Because I've lost whatever goodness I had inside me. In its place is a selfish sinner who doesn't even know up from down anymore. But I do know one thing. Tinkerbell makes me feel like I haven't felt in centuries. Alive and so fucking reckless, but also immensely peaceful. She makes me forget that I've been lost in this realm ever since I stepped foot here. And I'm not ready to give that up yet.

I'm not ready to give *her* up.

Chapter 16

Feelings by NIGHTBREAKERS

We're once again back at the docks. Sinful Delights is just a few blocks away but impossible to reach. After everything that happened with Hook last night, I'm feeling more unsettled than ever.

I don't belong at Sinful Delights. I know that now with full confidence. But do I belong on this ship? I thought that maybe I did, but now...I just don't know.

Hook stormed off the ship before we were even finished tying off. Again, his actions confuse the shit out of me. One second, he claims me, and the second, he can't get away fast enough. I had a sinking feeling in my chest as I watched him head into the city and out of sight. I know what he does when he visits his brother. He drinks and finds a girl to sleep with. We made a pretty clear-cut deal last night that neither one of us will sleep with anyone else until whatever is happening between us comes to an end. Will he keep his word? The way he practically ran off, I'm not entirely sure.

Huffing out a frustrated breath, I turn my back on the city and walk to the stern. Something I've come to realize since day one on this ship is that looking out over the endless sea to where it meets the sky is one of the most comforting things I've ever felt. In all reality, it should make me feel small and insignificant, but all I see is the beauty of it. The dark, mysterious ocean beneath me and the mesmerizing, hopeful sky above me. It sort of feels like me. The deepest, darkest parts of me are unknown, but for the first time since I can remember, I'm starting to feel hopeful.

I had a memory of who I was before I died. It's not much but it's something, and if I can remember that, then I know that I can remember more. And maybe once I finally remember who I am, I'll finally stop settling for the bare minimum. Maybe I'll finally believe that I'm worth more than what everyone seems to want to give me.

Sinn. Smee. Hook.

None of them want to actually give me anything. All they want to do is take. Take. Take. Take. As if I'm nothing more than an empty vessel that doesn't require anything of substance in return. And I guess I can't blame them. I've felt empty. I've acted empty. I've allowed myself to be treated this way because it's what I believe I deserve.

Letting out a heavy sigh, I lean against the rail and push those thoughts out of my head, trying to focus on nothing but the sun as it slowly descends.

"We should stop meeting this way," Sasha says as she sidles up next to me.

I glance sideways at her but keep my attention trained on the horizon. "Not like there are many choices on this ship."

"No, I suppose not. And this is as good as any."

I just nod, not entirely sure what to do or what to say. Red and Smee make it easy. Hell, even Killian is easy to be around. But Sasha is different. She doesn't have the same *come-near-me-and-I'll-punch-you-in-the-throat* attitude that I had, but she's not exactly an open door either. After a few minutes of not so comfortable silence, at least on my end, she finally reveals why she's sought me out.

"I've never seen him like this."

"Who?" I ask, even though I'm pretty sure I know who she's talking about.

"Oh, don't play coy. Not with me."

I grumble. "Fine. But I don't know what you want *me* to say about it."

"Well, you can start by admitting how you feel." She turns to face me, but I stubbornly keep my eyes locked forward. Her intense stare makes me want to squirm.

"He's just another typical, selfish asshole," I say, letting my anger at what happened last night fuel me. "He just happens to be a pretty asshole."

She snorts. "Don't let Smee hear you call anyone else pretty besides him."

Tilting my head to look at her, her sapphire eyes are sparkling like gems and she's fighting a smile. The amusement on her face causes my own to rise and I find myself also fighting a smile. Staring at each other, I feel like we're suddenly in church, sharing a secret and desperately trying not to laugh out loud. The idea only makes it that much harder. We both burst out laughing at the same time and it's exactly what I need.

"Thank you," I say through the lingering chuckles. "I needed that."

"I know," she says with a knowing gleam in her eyes. "It's what I do." When I look at her with confusion written all over my face, she clarifies. "Read people."

"Oh." My mind begins racing with professions that use that skill, trying to deduce what she did when she was alive. "Were you like, a body language expert or something?"

She smirks. "Or something. Though, I don't think being just a body language expert would land me in Purgatory with a one-way ticket to Hell."

"Oh," I repeat. "We don't have to—"

"Black Widow," she states plainly. "I was a Black Widow, though, it's a bit more complicated than that. There were a lot of rules involved and I was very particular about the cases I worked, but every single man I killed deserved it. Make no mistake about that."

Holy shit. I look at her in a new light, really look at her. I mean, she's gorgeous. I don't know any man that would see her and turn her down, especially if she was offering sex. But behind her beauty is a ruthless, intelligent killer. She'd have to be.

"How?" The question comes out before I can stop myself.

She smirks again, knowing exactly what I'm asking. "Poison. I never got my hands bloody. Too hard to get out of my nailbeds," she says as she looks down at her delicate hands. Lifting her eyes back up to me, she seems to examine me closely. "Enough about me. Back to my question."

Shaking my head, I sigh. "Honestly, I don't even know. One minute I think I see something between us and the next I'm quickly brought back to reality and knocked on my ass with the truth."

"Which is what?"

"He only wants me until he doesn't."

She hums in contemplation as she continues to examine me. "That's what you truly believe."

"That's what he said!" I practically shout my frustration.

"Did he actually say those words to you?" she asks.

Closing my eyes, I take a steadying breath and think back on our conversation in the tub. Not once did he say those exact words, but he didn't deny it either.

"No," I admit. "But he didn't argue against it when I laid it out plainly either. All he wants is sex. And in his words, he doesn't share. That's all this is, so it doesn't even matter how I feel."

She's silent for a few seconds before speaking again. "I can't speak in absolutes, but I can tell you what I see. I've been with Hook for a long time, and I've never seen him act like this. I pay attention to body language and facial features. I listen to meanings between words, both said and unsaid. I see the way you look at him. The way your body reacts to him."

Heat rushes up my neck and I scoff. "Everyone saw the way my body reacts to him."

She smiles and nods. "Yes, well, I can't deny the two shows you've both put on haven't made me a little envious." She bumps my shoulder playfully. "But that's both what I'm saying and not. The chemistry between you two is fucking intense, and not just when you're fucking. I see the way he watches you. The way he looks at you. Hell, the way he's already shown everyone that you're not to be touched. He can claim it's because he doesn't share or whatever, and maybe that's true, but it goes beyond that. This is deeper than just sex, for both of you. Whether each of you has realized that yet or not, well...." She shrugs.

"Even if what you're saying is true, having thoughts and feelings is one thing. Acting on them is another. But it's an entirely different thing to *admit* them."

"Yes. That's why I don't say anything is for certain. All I can say is what I know from my time with Hook and what I see. This is different. Where it leads will be up to the two of you." She turns to leave but places her hand on my shoulder. "If I can give you some advice?"

"Of course."

"Unless you enjoyed what happened last night, don't poke the bear. He may be an angel, but he's not above jealousy. Especially when *feelings* are involved." She winks and walks away, leaving me to further flounder in my thoughts, now more confusing than ever.

I watch the sunset before heading back to my room. The last thing I want right now is more eyes on me and more questions being thrown my way when I don't have even the slightest clue, much less answers. A quiet night alone to finish the book I started seems like the easiest and safest bet. I'm not up for another episode of last night's frozen shenanigans, no matter how good the sex was.

But when I finish my book and lie down to get some sleep, all I see is Hook's back as he raced off the ship, headed to Sinful Delights. Is he sleeping with someone right now? He's probably a bottle into his favorite rum and, just like Sinn, not thinking twice about me.

Chapter 17

Worship Me by Ari Abdul

Knock.

    Knock.

        Knock.

Sleep slowly fades away as the sound of distant knocking wakes me. The room is pitch black, letting me know that it's still the dead of night and I haven't been asleep for long. I don't even remember falling asleep.

    Knock.

        Knock.

            Knock.

Closing my eyes, I snuggle into the comforter. I'm not in the mood to be around anyone, not even Red's easy, cheery company. Whoever it is will go away if they think I'm asleep.

The knob turns and the door slowly opens, letting in a narrow beam of dim light. I'm positive I locked the door when I came in, so this can only be one person. Luckily, my back is to the door, so I just close my eyes and pretend to be asleep, hoping he leaves. But do I *really* want him to leave? A part of me does and a part of me doesn't. God, this is all so fucked up.

His quiet footsteps get closer and then the bed dips under his weight. "Tink, are you awake?"

His deep voice is quiet, but it still slides over me like a caress. Just this man's voice and my body comes alive. The scent of fresh night air and salt fills the room and I breathe deeply, but quietly, savoring it. His proximity is hard to ignore. Just like Sasha said, our chemistry is intense. We're like two magnets being pulled to each other by some unknown and unseen force. I fight to stay still, which is hard to do with my blood now pumping quickly through my veins. And when he slides the back of his knuckles down my exposed arm, goosebumps scatter across my skin, giving me away.

"Tink, I know you're awake. Can we talk?"

Squeezing my eyes shut, I try to prepare myself to face him, then slowly push up, sliding back to sit against the headboard. His body is framed by the light coming in from the hallway, leaving his face mostly lost to shadow. I can just make out the shine of his eyes as he looks at me.

"I don't think there's anything left to talk about," I say as I cross my arms protectively. As if that will stop him from getting to me.

He runs a hand down his face and then tugs at his beard. "What you said in the tub earlier...," he sighs, as if he's just as exhausted as I feel, "it's not like that. I don't like the way you made it sound."

I scoff. "The way I made it sound? It's the truth, Hook. It's not my fault you don't like the way truth sounds. Lies are always prettier."

"You make it seem like I'm the villain here. Like I just want to use you and then throw you away when I'm done with you."

"Isn't that what you're doing?"

"No, I...fuck."

He gets up and starts pacing, hands sliding through his hair. Even in this dim light, his body is amazing. The way the light shines off the leather of his pants, showcasing his muscular thighs. He's wearing one of his corset-style vests again, only this time, there's no shirt underneath. His incredible arms are on full display, giving me flashes of color and muscle as he walks back and forth next to the bed.

"I don't know what will happen in the future. I can't promise you something that I'm not certain of. I mean, I could, but it would be a lie. And I don't want to lie to you, Tink." He stops pacing and returns to the bed, this time lifting a knee to the mattress and leaning into me.

"Unless you want to hear pretty lies? Tell me what you want to hear, Tink. I'll say whatever you want. But the truth is, when I see you, I have the intense need to touch you. And it's not a need I want to control. I *want* to touch you, Tinkerbell."

He reaches out and grabs my arm, pulling it free. "And I want you to touch me," he says as he places my hand on his chest. "I want to kiss you and get lost in you. I want to hear that beautiful voice of yours moan and cry out as I make your body sing. I want those incredible hazel eyes locked on me when they're hooded and lost to pleasure. I don't want to hide this, and I don't want to second-guess it. I just want to be able to act on this…this fucking *urge* I have when I'm around you."

His heart pounds against my palm as he leans in closer. His eyes dart back and forth between mine almost frantically. As if he's desperate to see understanding and acceptance in mine.

"That's the truth, Tink. I don't know anything else beyond that. All I know is what I feel in this moment, and I think you feel it too. So, can we just live in this moment? Is that too much to ask?"

He cradles my face in his hand, his thumb slowly tracing my bottom lip, causing me to suck in a breath. When he's this close to me, when he's touching me, I can't think straight. I don't want to think straight. Maybe what he's saying makes the most sense out of any other scenario. Maybe I need to stop thinking for once in my life and just act on what I want. Because if I do what I want, regardless of what happens, at least I won't have any regrets.

His eyes drop to my mouth and he lowers his head. His breath is warm against my lips, and I can smell the rum on his breath as he whispers, "Can we just think about right now and do what our bodies want to do without thinking about tomorrow?"

It's so very clear what we both want to do. Pushing away all my thoughts, worries, doubts, and what-ifs, I give in to the moment and whisper, "Yes."

He releases a heavy sigh, sinking further onto the bed and over me as his lips land on mine. He holds our lips together, just a simple kiss, but I feel his body relax into it, as if this is what he's been waiting for all night. Then he pulls back, slowly rubbing his bottom lip back and forth on mine before pressing his lips down firmly again. Unlike any of our other kisses, this feels unhurried, as if we have all the time in the world to explore every sensation.

He pulls back again, this time licking along my bottom lip before pulling it into his mouth and gently biting. My chest constricts and a deep whimper escapes my throat. His hand, still cradling my cheek, gently tilts my head to the side and he finally sweeps his tongue against mine. I slide my hands up his chest and around his neck, into his long hair.

He moans into my mouth, taking the kiss even deeper, but keeps his pace agonizingly slow. It's delicious and maddening. It's the first time either one of us has held back from literally devouring each other. Being able to focus on just this kiss is intoxicating. I've never been kissed so intently, so thoroughly before, and it has my heart sinking and soaring at the same time.

All too soon, he's pulling back, breaking the best kiss of my life before I want it to end. "Not here," he says, breathless.

"What?" My mind is still processing that kiss and I don't understand what he's saying.

"This bed is way too small and can't handle what I want to do to you. Come on." He climbs off the bed and takes my hand, pulling me out of the covers.

I follow eagerly as he leads me down the hallway toward his room. I don't know where the crew is, or even if they're still awake, but I'm thankful we don't run into anyone. Not that they haven't already seen the show, but I don't want this spell I'm currently under to be broken.

When his bedroom door clicks shut and locks behind us, he turns to face me. The air is charged, practically crackling with electricity as we eye fuck each other. There's no denying what Sasha said, our attraction is palpable. But as I'm standing here staring at this sexy man, knowing full well what's to come, I can't help but think about the past two nights. How he put me on display and made me crawl to him. How he tied me up. I've literally been at his mercy.

"What's that look? Did you change your mind?" Hook asks as he eyes me nervously.

"No, I haven't changed my mind." I shake my head. "But I am a bit frustrated with how the past two nights have gone. I'm not saying I didn't enjoy what we did, well…minus the freezing part but…," I shrug, "I don't know. You wanted truth and the truth is, I guess I'm just a little salty about it."

He approaches me slowly, closing the distance between us. He reaches for my wrists and brings them to his lips, softly kissing each one where they're raw and tender from the ropes cutting into the skin.

"Let me make it up to you. Just tell me what you want, and I'll do it. Whatever you want, it's yours."

Chewing on my bottom lip, I contemplate his offer. What do I want right now, in this moment? I want Hook, obviously. But I want to feel like I'm the only other soul in the world. No crew watching us. Nothing to distract his attention. I want to be his sole focus and I want him to worship me.

Looking up into his handsome face, I see the sincerity of his offer. So, let's see if he means it. "I want you to beg for my forgiveness and not with your words. I want my body to be your altar and I want you to worship before me. And…I want to believe you mean it."

Trailing his fingertips from my wrists, up my arms, over my shoulders and lightly up my neck, before he takes my face in his hands and kisses me again. Just like the one before, it's slow and deep. I realize the way he's kissing me tonight is already proof that he has no problem with what I asked. His kiss. His touch. It's reverent.

His lips leave my mouth to trail along my jaw. I tilt my head to the side, giving him better access to my neck as he lays soft, open mouth kisses down to my shoulder. He moves the thin strap of my shirt to the side, continuing his slow perusal of my skin. His warm tongue slips out and glides across my collarbone before his lips skim back up my throat, and he kisses me again.

When his hands slide down and grab the bottom of my shirt, lifting, I don't stop him. Tossing the shirt aside, he continues to explore my body with his lips and tongue and teeth. His large hands wrap around my waist, squeezing gently as he sucks a nipple into his mouth and flicks it with his tongue. I let out a moan that turns into a hiss when he bites down, but quickly releases it, and continues kissing a trail down my stomach.

On his knees in front of me, he hooks his fingers into my shorts and slides them down my legs. I hold on to his shoulders as I step out of them, and they're tossed aside as well. His hands run up the back of my thighs and I shudder at the sensation of his calloused hands against my soft skin.

He looks up at me and there's no mistaking the heat in his eyes. It's clear that he finds me attractive and wants to fuck me. Seeing this look in his eyes, directed at me, gives me all the confidence in the world to stand naked before him and not get in my head.

"Truth?" he asks, breaking our silence. I nod. "That night on deck, I was terrified you were going to run in the opposite direction.

But then you upped the stakes and undressed before crawling to me, and I didn't see embarrassment or shame in your eyes. I saw power. I swear I forgot how to breathe. Because I didn't see the cold, angry Tinkerbell. I saw a goddess and worshipping is what you deserve."

And with that, his hands slide up to cup my ass and he pulls me forward. I gasp as his warm mouth claims my pussy. And when his wet tongue slides between my lips and finds my clit, I close my eyes, throw my head back, and moan. His beard tickles and scrapes against my sensitive skin, giving me more sensations to drive me towards the edge of ecstasy.

Pushing my hands in his hair to help steady myself, I look back down and find him already watching me. God, he looks good on his knees, face between my legs, and the brightest aqua eyes taking in every reaction.

"Fuck, that feels good," I exclaim, voice already breathy.

When my legs start to shake, he moves his arms under my thighs, wrapping them securely around me to help hold me up. This position opens my legs wider and allows him to dive deeper inside of me. His expert tongue licks and flicks and caresses, while his lips and mouth suck and bite.

My breathing is heavy, and my moans and whimpers are loud in the otherwise quiet room. My body is shaking so much I feel unsteady on my feet. Only Hook's strong hold keep me standing.

"I'm so close. Fuck, Hook, I'm gonna cum."

He moans with his mouth still locked on my pussy. I try to keep my eyes open, to watch his face as I cum, but it's too intense. My eyes squeeze shut, legs squeeze together, and hands grip into his hair, desperate to hold on to something as my entire body spasms and vibrates through my orgasm.

The next thing I register is the soft mattress underneath me. When I open my eyes, Hook is standing at the edge of the bed, eyes heated as they rake over my body, and hand rubbing his hard dick pressed against his pants. I suddenly have another request.

"I want to see you."

"You have seen me."

I shake my head and lift up onto my elbows. "No, I want to *really* see you. I want you to undress in front of me and let me take my time looking at you. I want to see you stroke yourself as you think about fucking me."

He reaches behind his back and pulls the ties on his corset, loosening it, and then his fingers slowly but deftly unhook the buttons running down the front. Once it's open, he slides it off his shoulders and tosses it somewhere along with my clothes on the floor.

Then his hands release the button on his pants, the zipper, and he's peeling the leather down his legs and stepping out of them. Once he's standing in front of me completely naked, my heart skips a few beats.

He's devastating.

Broad round shoulders that look like they could hold up the entire world. Arms that are almost as thick as my legs, veins running up his forearms that drive me feral. A solid chest that accentuates a tapered waist and the most defined eight-pack I've ever seen. He even has those sexy ass muscles along his rib cage, whatever they're called. But over all of that delicious skin and muscle are tattoos.

Colorful pictures, designs, and swirls of ink cover every inch of his skin, from his wrists to his shoulders, down his chest and stomach, and onto his legs. They don't stop until they reach his ankles. His hands are left free of ink, but his fingers are all adorned with silver and gems. They sparkle and glint in the lights as he strokes his hard cock.

A cock that matches the rest of him. Big. Perfectly symmetrical. A defined head that's a lighter shade of pink than the rest, with a thick vein running from base to tip underneath. A vein I want to trace with my tongue before taking him in my mouth.

Fuck.

Between the orgasm, watching him stroke himself, and the thought of sucking his dick, I'm soaking wet. I can feel it dripping out my pussy.

"I need you," I admit, my voice squeezed tight with anticipation. "Please, Hook. Come and fuck me."

Without hesitation, he climbs onto the bed, holding himself over me. My legs open and wrap around him, allowing him access. I reach for his arms, caressing my way up them until I grip his triceps. God, he's so solid. Every inch of him is fucking perfect.

"You know…." He caresses my cheek with his thumb, his eyes roaming over my face in awe. "You shine so bright under the attention of the crew, but you've never looked as beautiful as you do right now, with only my eyes on you. I'm prepared to spend all night worshipping your body. Kissing every inch of you. Making you cum again and again. I don't need to fuck you to bring you pleasure."

His words cause emotion to swell in my chest and I have to fight against the thick ball of emotion threatening to ruin me. "Please," I beg, reaching between our bodies.

My hand wraps around his hard dick, causing Hook to groan and close his eyes. I stroke him, amazed at how hard and soft he is at the same time. Lifting my hips slightly, I rub the head of his cock against my pussy.

"Can't you feel how wet I am? I need you, Hook. I need you inside me."

His eyes lock on mine and whatever he sees on my face is enough to satisfy him. Without another word, he pushes his hips forward. The tip of his dick stretching me open makes me gasp, but it's cut short as Hook's mouth lands on mine. He pushes into me just as slowly as he kisses me. I can feel every inch of him sliding into me, forcing my body open for him, until it feels like he's so deep his dick could touch my belly button.

He holds still for a minute, sheathed all the way inside me. "Jesus, you're so fucking tight." He grits his teeth.

Then he starts to move. His large dick sliding in and out of me feels like nothing else I've ever felt. Hook's large body dominating me but also savoring me is what Heaven must be like. I moan and whimper underneath him, hands reaching for his sculpted ass as I pull him into me, my hips moving to meet his thrusts. Demanding more.

He breaks the kiss to hold himself up higher, pushing in harder and faster. "You feel so good, Tink. Fuck."

We're both breathing heavy, and our eyes lock, and nothing else matters. Just this moment. And God, is this moment fucking amazing.

I move my hands to hold on to his massive thighs. "More. Give me more."

He slams into me, causing me to arch my back and cry out. But I can tell he's still holding back. He's held back every time we've been together. Even when he was angry and tied me up, I knew he was in control. I don't want him to be in control. I want him to fuck me like he wants to fuck me.

"Harder," I demand.

He shakes his head. "I don't want to hurt you."

"You're not going to break me," I say, holding his gaze. "Stop controlling yourself, get out of your head, and fuck me like you mean it."

"I don't—"

"I want it. I need it too, Hook. Please."

He sits up on his knees and grabs my thighs, holding them open wide and when he slams into me, I see fucking stars. My body scoots up the bed and I reach behind me, bracing myself against the headboard.

"Holy fuck," I pant. His dick hits a glorious spot deep inside me and I feel the orgasm building.

The room is filled with the sounds of our fucking. Flesh slapping against flesh. Moans and cries and curses. It's the sexiest thing I've ever heard.

"I'm gonna cum, Hook. Don't stop."

The sounds, the visual, the feel of Hook slamming into me, his grip on my thighs, and the look in his eyes, have me launching over the edge in the hardest orgasm I've ever had. My pussy throbs and clenches around his dick for what feels like minutes, my orgasm unrelenting as I soak his cock with my release. Just as my orgasm starts to fade, Hook's voice echoes my own.

"I'm gonna cum."

He falls to his hands as he thrusts one last time. I reach down and grab his ass again, pulling him in deep as he follows me over the edge. His dick pulses inside me and his arms shudder as they continue to hold him through his own intense orgasm.

We're left panting together, his head dropped onto my shoulder as we come down from Heaven together. After a few seconds, he pulls out of me and collapses on the bed beside me. Looking over at him, a lazy satisfied grin pulls at his lips, and I can't help but mirror it.

"That was…." He trails off, closing his eyes and exhaling.

"Yeah," I agree.

As our breathing settles, the silence between us stretches, and then gets heavy. I realize I'm in his bed, in his room, and just like last time, he probably doesn't want me to stay here.

Clearing my throat, I push up into a sitting position. "Well, I guess I'll go."

He nods. "Okay."

And just like that, the plummet from Heaven is met with the hard impact of the ground. My heart sinks in my chest and I have to fight the emotion that swells, threatening to spill down my cheeks. I hate that he affects me like this. I agreed to do this. I knew the rules. And still, I have no control over my damn heart.

I don't waste any time dressing. I don't want to be in his room a second longer than necessary, afraid I'll lose control and cry in front of him. So, I just pick up my discarded clothes, hold them to my chest, and practically run for the door. It doesn't matter if I walk back to my room naked anyways. It's nothing the crew hasn't already seen. But as I open the door, I scan the hallway before walking out. I may not care about being seen naked, but I sure as hell don't want to be caught doing the walk of shame.

The hallway blurs as I step into it. I'm trying desperately not to let the tears fall until I'm safely locked behind my bedroom door, but I'm failing.

"Wait."

Hook's voice makes me flinch and I walk faster. I don't want him to see me like this. He wouldn't understand it and I can't explain it to him because I don't fully understand it.

A strong arm wraps around my waist, stopping my escape, and he whispers in my ear, "Stay."

And just like that, one word, and I break. The tears cascade down my cheeks and a choked sob escapes my throat. Then, I'm once again in his arms as he carries me back to his room. I hide my face in his chest while I fight back the tears. He doesn't say anything as he lays me down in his bed, taking the clothes from my arms, and pulling the covers over my body. He reaches down to gently wipe the tears from my cheeks and I close my eyes, slightly turning away from him. I hate that he's seeing me like this.

He doesn't say a word as he turns the lights off and then slides into bed behind me. He once again wraps me up in his arms and pulls me against him. He molds his large body flush against mine and holds on to me tightly. He plants a soft kiss to my shoulder and then sinks onto the pillow next to me.

I feel his body relax, his chest rising and falling against my back as his breathing evens out and he falls asleep. Only when I hear a soft snore do I let myself relax in his hold. I let out a shaky exhale, my body and mind suddenly feeling exhausted.

The past two days feel like I've been at an amusement park. Literally on and off rides, throwing my body and emotions this way and that way and upside down. I don't know which way is up and which way is down. I don't know what to think. I don't know what to do.

Mercifully, sleep pulls me under, and I fall into a deep, dreamless sleep.

Chapter 18

Call Me Yours by A Foreign Affair

I knew as soon as I said okay last night that it was the wrong thing to say. Not just because I saw the pain in her eyes, but because I felt that same pain in my chest.

I'm not used to this.

I'm not used to second-guessing myself. I'm not used to feeling conflicted. This past week has been an eye-opener for me. Well, more like a punch in the face. Sure, I love my crew and have a fondness for the souls I ferry, but I've never felt *this* before.

As much strife as I've given Peter about being cold and empty, I realize now that I've been the same way. I'm not a complete miserable bastard like he is, but when it comes to the deep shit, I've avoided it just the same. I've pushed it down and masked it behind jokes and laughter. No one has ever cracked my exterior, much less gotten inside.

Until Tink.

I feel like my chest has been sliced open. I feel vulnerable. As if she could wrap her small hand around my heart and yank it right out of my chest to do with as she pleases. And knowing someone has that kind of hold on you…is terrifying.

Thinking of her small hand, the way it looked and felt wrapped around my hard dick, makes me moan. Falling asleep with her in my arms, feeling her soft, naked body pressed against mine, has left me wound tight and horny, even in my sleep. I've been dreaming about her since the first night she spent on this ship, but this dream feels better than all the others.

Consciousness comes slowly and then all at once as I realize this isn't a dream at all. The bed is still warm next to me, but Tink is no longer lying beside me.

Grabbing the comforter, I throw it back, revealing Tink kneeling between my legs. Both of her small hands wrapped around my hard dick, twisting and stroking. Her eyes meet mine, a mischievous and heated look matching her devious grin. She licks the tip of my cock, her tongue circling around and around, lips grazing but never closing around me.

"Good morning," she says innocently, as if she's not teasing the shit out of me.

"Little viper," I reply, voice gravely with sleep and lust.

She lowers her head and licks me slowly from base to tip, where precum is already glistening from my excitement. She licks it, and then finally slides me into her mouth, moaning as she tastes me.

"Fuck." I pull the extra pillow over and throw an arm behind my head, propping myself up to watch her.

This is the best fucking thing I've ever woken up to. All of this feels surreal. Her in my arms. Me inside her tight little pussy. Her beautiful lips stretched around my cock. And the swell of something heavy in my chest.

Her hair is a mess, and although short on the sides, it's still long enough on top to fall across her face. I want to see her. Reaching down with my free hand, I hold it back, letting my hand rest on her head as she bobs up and down.

"Look at me." Not a demand this time. A request.

Large hazel eyes sparkle up at me, more honey than green in the dim light of the room.

"God, you're beautiful."

She moans around my dick, the vibration sending a shiver up

my spine. She keeps one hand stroking my dick, following in the wake of her mouth, and the other she uses to caress my balls, squeezing and pulling and rubbing.

"Goddamn it, Tink," I growl out, lifting my hips to thrust into her mouth as I hold her head, feeling my dick hit the back of her throat.

I push harder, slipping down the tightness of her throat, and she gags but keeps on going. Jesus Christ. Tinkerbell gagging on my cock is the sexiest thing I've ever seen.

"If you don't want my cum in your mouth, stop right now," I manage to warn her.

She rolls her eyes up to look at me, tears streaking down her cheeks, but she grips my dick tighter with her hand and sucks harder. My entire body tenses up, my abs constricting almost painfully. "Fuuck," I groan as I cum down her throat. She continues to stroke and suck until I sag against the bed, my hand falling away from her head.

She moans one last time as she finally slides my dick out of her mouth. When she licks her lips and smiles up at me, for the second time in as many nights, I forget how to breathe. When her eyes shine with such raw, feminine power and light, it knocks me off my feet. It makes me wonder why she was ever anything different. Why was she such a cold and dark version of herself for so long? I want to know everything about her so I can never let that happen again.

She throws me off when she climbs out of bed instead of sliding up to cuddle with me, like I expected her to. Like I wanted her to do.

"What are the chances that I can get some more of those delicious Hook pancakes?" she asks with a bright smile as she dresses in her clothes from the night before.

"Really?" I ask incredulously. "*That's* what you're thinking about right now?"

She nods. "I'm starving. I skipped dinner last night."

My body feels heavy, satiated, and relaxed. The last thing I want to do right now is climb out of bed, but I force myself up. She says she's starving but so am I, just not for food. I'm hungry for more of her. Still completely naked, I walk over to her, tip her chin up, and lean down for a kiss when she turns her head away.

"I just gave you head," she mutters.

Gripping her chin tighter, I pull her back to me. "And?"

"And...," she swallows, "don't you think that's gross?"

I can't help the smile that pulls one side of my mouth. "I can get all up in your pussy and expect you to kiss me afterwards but it's gross when you do it? Cum is cum. Mine or yours, it doesn't matter."

I press my mouth to hers and demand entry with my tongue. She finally concedes and lets me in. Honestly, the taste of myself on her tongue is heady. I pull her closer and she tiptoes, reaching for me. Before I know it, I'm lifting, and her legs wrap tight around my waist as the kiss gets hotter and deeper. I want to walk her back to the bed and undress her, spend my morning eating her and fucking her, but knowing that she's hungry stops me.

I end the kiss and slowly release her. She slides down my body until she's once again standing.

"Then again, who needs food," she teases.

"You do. And that's not up for discussion. I've noticed you don't eat much and are always skipping meals. That's going to change," I say as I walk into the closet.

She scoffs. "Okay, Dad."

"Joke all you want but I'm serious. If you're not going to take care of yourself, then I will."

When she turns to face me again, I watch as her eyes slowly rake down my body. She bites her lip, and an adorable blush flushes her cheeks.

"Jesus," she mumbles under her breath.

"No, just an angel."

"Are you going out there like that?"

I look down at my exposed upper body and grey sweatpants. "What's wrong with this?"

She shakes her head rapidly. "Nothing. Nothing is wrong with any of that but...I mean, the crew."

"We've all seen each other naked at this point, Tink. Come on." I grab her hand and pull her out of the room.

"I think you underestimate the power of grey sweatpants," she says all breathy behind me.

I chuckle, feeling lighthearted and at ease in her presence again. Things are definitely different, but it feels good not to have to hold anything back.

"Any other requests besides pancakes?" I ask as I start rummaging through the fridge and cabinets.

"Bacon, obviously. And eggs. Scrambled eggs. How can I help?"

She can't hide the happiness and excitement practically jumping out of her. The smile on her face and the light in her eyes make me want to selfishly take her back to my room but also do more of this. Whatever it takes to keep this look on her face.

Setting down a handful of ingredients on the counter, I walk back to her and lift her up, sitting her on the island. I have the urge to kiss her again, and so, I do. This is exactly what I was talking about last night. I don't want to hold myself back from her.

"You just sit here and look beautiful. Maybe sing a song if you're up for it." I chuck her chin and then head back to the task of making breakfast.

"What song do you want to hear?"

I shrug. "Sing whatever comes to you."

She's quiet for a few seconds but then she starts to sing a

song that feels like she plucked right out of my head, *Hungry Eyes*. The swell in my chest is almost suffocating. I have to lean against the counter to collect myself. Her voice is pure harmony. It's smooth and strong, honed to perfection. Her tone is slightly raspy, and it reminds me of when she's lost in pleasure beneath me.

Fuck. Everything she does affects me. I'm trying so hard not to fall for her, but I think that ship has sailed. If the rest of my life is made up of nights like last night and mornings like today, I'd have no complaints.

But how long will I remain here? My goal has always been to go back home. When? Or how? I don't know, but that's always been my future. I think that's why I've never cared to truly bond with anyone. To build a relationship that I didn't want to leave behind. Because this crew is stuck in the Land of Never. They failed to cross into their Afterlife a long time ago and now The Gates are sealed to them forever.

Including Tink.

"Mm, I smell pancakes!" Red squeals in delight as she comes barreling into the kitchen, interrupting my negative thoughts. "He never makes pancakes twice in one week. This must be your doing," she addresses Tink as she jumps onto the island to sit next to her. "So, how was your night?"

I don't need to turn around to know Tink has a blush creeping into her cheeks at the innocent question. It makes me smirk just thinking about it. She's so shy in front of the crew for the simplest things, but yet she's a fucking powerhouse when she's naked. It's a crazy juxtaposition but I love it about her.

Before I know it, the entire crew has made their way into the kitchen and it's a chorus of small talk and laughter as I finish breakfast.

"Breakfast is ready," I announce.

I serve two plates full of food and walk over to the island, setting them down next to each other. I take a seat in a barstool and Tink hops off the island, moving to sit in the one next to mine.

"Uh-uh." I grab her by the waist and lift her onto my lap. "This is your seat." I can tell she's a bit uneasy. I whisper in her ear while everyone is still busy serving themselves. "I said I didn't want to think about acting on what I want, and this is what I want. I want everyone to see you with me. I want everyone to know that you're mine. But mostly, I just want to be able to feel you and touch you." I playfully bite her neck, smirking when I see goosebumps scatter across her skin. "Now eat."

I have to admit it isn't the easiest way to eat breakfast, when someone is in your lap, but I managed, easily fielding questions and comments from the crew.

"So," Sasha points her fork at us, "this is a thing then?"

"It is," I say easily, noticing a quiet exchange happening between Sasha and Tink.

"I think it's nice," Fin comments, before quickly ducking his head and returning his attention to his food.

"Which means, hands off, I take it?" Smee asks.

"It does." I can't help the rumble in my voice. The thought of him or anyone touching Tink in a sexual way makes me incredibly furious.

Smee sighs heavily. "You never let me have any fun."

I scoff. "Fun is all you have, Smee. There will be new souls on board tonight."

Killian remains utterly quiet, but then again, that's not uncommon. Still, I don't forget that Tink seemed to have chosen him, climbing into his lap before I stopped her from going further. I wonder if there's something there. I'll be watching that possibility closely.

"I suppose I can't complain. Gotta let you have at least one," Smee winks and continues to eat his breakfast.

All I can do is shake my head at his utter nonsense. He pokes and argues but he'll obey my rules just as much as the rest of them will. One thing we all have for each other is mutual respect.

"You guys look so cute together," Red says with a beaming smile. "And I absolutely am pulling the BFF card and getting all the juicy details later."

Tink's face is flushed from all the attention, but I'm happy to see that most of her food is gone and she seems to still be glowing and not shutting down.

"We need to prepare the ship for transport today. There are a few crates that will be delivered this afternoon to store before the souls board. If you need me, you know where to find me, but I highly suggest that you don't need me until the souls are ready to board," I say, getting to my feet and taking Tink's hand again. "No one come into the bathroom for the next hour."

"Oo, scrub-a-dub-dub," Red singsongs.

"Hook getting fucked in the tub," Smee continues.

We walk out of the kitchen to whistles and more taunts, but nothing they say or do fazes me anymore. I know it's going to take Tink a while to get used to their constant teasing and prodding, but she will. And to reward her for eating her food, handling it all so well, and for this morning's pleasurable wake-up call, I plan on making her cum until she can't cum anymore.

Chapter 19

Euphoria by Colorblind

The past two weeks have flown by! Or is it three? Time doesn't really apply to ship life and that concept is actually quite relieving. I'm surprised at how much I've changed in such a short period of time. To say I had a rocky start is an understatement, but I've since gained my sea-legs and my place on the crew. At least, it feels like I have.

Red mentioned that it felt the same way to her when she came on this ship. It's like finding that last puzzle piece. The immense satisfaction of hearing it click into place and seeing the entire picture come to life.

Or I could literally just be lost in a love-drunk phase. Not love, love. Like, I don't *love* Hook. I'm not *in love* with him. Jesus, why am I saying the word love so much? Hook and I haven't talked about anything more since we both agreed to just live in the moment, so that's what I'm doing. Anyway, it's just been oddly….

Perfect.

I've taken it upon myself to swab the deck full-time. Not surprising, no one fought me on it. The task has become cathartic for me. There's something calming and rewarding about the quiet push/pull of the broom across the deck. The exercise has also been good for me, toning me up, which I need after all the delicious food Hook feeds me.

I can't remember a time I ever felt so at ease. At peace. I still don't have any more insight into my life before Purgatory, but it's mattering less and less. I'm happy with the woman I'm becoming despite not knowing my life before. And who I was at Sinful Delights gets further and further away every time we sail out of port.

We're back once again though and we just tied off. Looking out on to the land that I was forced to leave, I no longer feel any longing for what I had before. I no longer have any desire or urge to leave the ship. I want to be here. I want to explore this life with the crew. I want to explore what the future could possibly hold...with Hook.

"Do you wish you could go back?" Hook's voice interrupts my thoughts as he steps up behind me, wrapping me up in his strong arms.

"Surprisingly...no." I turn in his hold to face him. "I was just thinking that, actually. That this is the first time since leaving that no part of me wants to go back. Not even a little." I slide my hands up his chest and around his neck, tiptoeing to bring my face closer to his. The uncertainty in his blue eyes nags at me. "I'm exactly where I want to be," I assure him.

He nips at my lips. "Good."

"Although, you are in my way of watching the sunset. You make a better door than a window, you know."

"I can be better than a door or a window." His wings emerge from behind his back, catching me off guard.

I gasp and gawk at their beauty. I've seen them almost every day for the past...however long, and I'm still not used to their etherealness.

"Would you like to watch the sunset from above the clouds, little viper?"

I snap my eyes back up to his. "Seriously?!"

He chuckles. "Yes, seriously. Do you trust me to fly you up?"

"Are you kidding?" I mock. "I trust you with my life."

His satisfied grin sends my heart racing as he scoops me into his arms and turns around, walking a few steps away from the railing. Then, his massive wings beat against the air, and we gracefully ascend into the sky, sending my heart sinking into my stomach. Looking down, I watch as the ship shrinks below us until we're in the clouds and it's no longer visible. Only then do I turn my face out to the open sky. I open my mouth to say something, but nothing comes out. I'm left utterly speechless at the sight before me.

There's a bite in the air, the first real glimpse of winter approaching, but I barely notice the cold. Thick, fluffy clouds blanket the sky below us like a floor made out of cotton balls. Reaching my arm out, I try to touch them as we fly through wisps, but they seem to disappear right through my fingers. And the colors? I've never seen anything so vivid before. It's like the most vibrant oil paints have been glazed and shine with intensity. I wish I could capture this sight, but I know no photo or painting would ever come close to the real thing.

"It's beautiful, isn't it?" Hook's quiet whisper penetrates my trance.

"It's…." I don't even know the word to describe it. I don't think there is a word to describe it. "Beautiful doesn't seem like the right word. It's…exquisite. It's…Heavenly."

We glide smoothly toward the horizon as the sun sets. Just like all the other times I've watched the sunset, it's over much too quickly. The colors linger but slowly start to lose their vibrancy.

"You're cold," Hook states, worry in his tone.

"A little," I agree, finally feeling my body shiver from the cold air rushing across my skin.

He hugs me tighter to his chest, and I cling to him as we descend. Dropping below the clouds, the dark sea is endless below us. Even from way up here, I feel so incredibly small in the world. I glance around, not seeing the ship anywhere in sight. Instead, a small island catches my attention with a hidden cove of the bluest waters

I've ever seen. Turquoise, just like Hook's eyes.

He lands us softly at the edge of the water. My feet sink into soft white sand as he sets me down.

"What is this place?" I ask in wonder, taking in the serenity of the secluded beach.

"This is the Mermaid Lagoon."

Taking a step closer to Hook, I reach for him. "Why would you bring me here? You know my deal with Serene."

"Your deal with Serene is being fulfilled. There's no reason to worry. C'mon, get undressed," he says as he starts to remove his own clothing.

I glance around nervously.

"They're not here," he assures me. "They only come here when they need replenishing and healing. No one else is allowed to use these waters except for me and Peter. And, because you're with me, now you."

"I'm sure they're not going to be happy about you making that decision."

He chuckles again. "I'm an angel, they're mermaids, and this is literally my brother's realm. They don't really get to dictate what we do." He steps up to me, gently tilting my chin and capturing my gaze. "Besides, I would never let anything happen to you." He reaches for my shirt and starts to lift but stops before getting too far. "Do you trust me?"

Giving in, I nod. I don't know if it's good judgement on my part or not, but I *do* trust him. Once he's undressed me, he takes my hand and leads me into the water.

"It's warm!" I beam up at him, excited.

"Of course it is. You think I was going to have you get into cold water after you were already cold?"

"You said the mermaids come back to replenish and heal.

Does that mean this water is magical? Does it have healing properties?"

"Amongst other things."

When the water is waist high, he releases my hand to dive underneath. He emerges a few feet away, running his hands through his hair to slick it back. I'm grateful to be wading in the water because the sight makes my knees weak.

"Come here." He curls his pointer finger, beckoning me forward.

Once the water reaches my shoulders, I sink under and swim the rest of the way. My hands find his stomach and I surface in front of him. His hands immediately find my ass and hold me as I wrap my legs around his waist and arms around his neck. Our eyes clash and I'm held hostage in their depth. I could seriously look into his eyes every day for the rest of my life and never get used to their beauty. My heart is already thundering inside me at the feel of his naked body pressed against mine. It doesn't take long before I feel his hard dick rubbing against me and my gaze drops to his lips.

"Do you want to fuck me in the warm healing waters of the Mermaid Lagoon, little viper?"

"Yes," I breathe out immediately.

"Do you have a thing for Killian?"

My eyes are back on his, confusion furrowing my eyebrows. "What?"

"Answer the question. Do you want Killian?"

"What? God, no. Where is this even coming from?

"What about Peter? Are you in love with my brother and only using me to get back at him?"

I rear back as if he's physically struck me. "You really think I'd do that?"

"Please, just answer."

"No. The answer is no, to *all* of those questions. I don't understand what's happening."

Hook clamps down on his jaw as if he's trying hard not to provide an answer.

"Hook, why would you ask me these questions?"

He lets out a heavy sigh. "For obvious reason about my brother, and because of what I saw in the kitchen, and then when I pulled you out of Killian's lap. It's been on my mind, and I wasn't going to fully give up that line of thinking until I knew for sure."

I'm hurt that he's even been thinking this way, that he could think I'd use him like that, but another part of me finds it rather reassuring. A slow smile starts to pull at my lips when I understand the underlying reasons for his questions. "Were you…jealous?"

He grimaces, but answers. "Yes."

"I know most people think jealousy is a bad thing." I shrug. "But I don't. It means you care. And I think it's sweet," I say as I move in to claim his mouth. Before the kiss gets too heated, I pull back. "Why did you ask me this now? You literally could have asked me any time and I would have told you."

"Fuck, this is backfiring," he grumbles.

I laugh. "What is?"

He sighs. "The waters. You asked if they had healing properties and I said amongst other things. They also allow one only to speak the truth."

My eyebrows shoot up in surprise. "Oh." As the surprise wears off, the heavy reality of our current situation sinks in. "Ohhh."

He nods. "Don't ask questions you don't really want to know the answers to."

I swallow, suddenly incredibly nervous. "This is dangerous."

"Yes," he whispers against my lips, rubbing his dick against my pussy. "But you still want to fuck me."

"Yes," I admit, letting him kiss me, but now my mind is racing. I pull back again. "Have you ever brought anyone else here?"

"No."

"Why did you bring me?"

He hesitates for only a second. "Because I want to share everything with you, Tink."

I don't know how *not* to read into that statement. I want to share everything with you. That's not something you say to just anyone. Everything means literally everything. A life together. But everything could mean something entirely different to him than it does to me. Right?

"You don't...." I look into his eyes, suddenly feeling unsteady and vulnerable. "You don't want to be done with me?"

"I don't think I'm *ever* going to be done with you."

Another surprised gasp leaves my lips as his wings appear behind him. He's never had them out during sex. When I asked if I could touch them before, he immediately hid them away with a resounding, *no*. I hesitate.

"Touch them."

My eyes dart back and forth between his, still questioning his offer, but all I see is openness and sincerity in his eyes. There's not one ounce of resignation.

Slowly, I let my fingers reach out to them. They look like beautiful white wisps of light, like I can push my hand right through them, but that's not the case at all. They're solid under my fingertips and softer than anything I've ever felt.

Hook shivers as I gently caress his wings, and when I glance back at his face, his eyes are closed and there's a look of pure bliss on his face. Then he opens his eyes again, meeting mine. The air is heavy around us, my entire body heating up from the inside out, and I struggle to find words.

Finally, all I can manage is a soft, "Thank you."

Thank you for trusting me. Thank you for sharing this place with me. Thank you for seeing me. Thank you for so much more than I can ever say.

And with that, he silences any more unnecessary words with a kiss I don't ever want to break free from. I cling to him like my life depends on it. Like if he lets me go in the lagoon right now, I'd sink to the bottom and drown. It feels like I'm close to drowning anyway. Fighting against a current of emotion that's so strong, if I'm not careful, it's going to pull me under.

He lifts me up with one hand on my ass while the other positions his dick at my opening. When he slowly lowers me down, I throw my head back and moan my pleasure to the sky. He uses both his hands to grip my ass and control my body, lifting me up and down his cock.

The water makes me feel weightless and I relish the feel of it surrounding us like a warm blanket, small waves rippling away from our bodies as we make another beautiful song to add to our playlist.

Hook kisses and sucks on my neck before leaning down to give my breasts attention. When his tongue flicks my nipple, it sends a bolt of desire down my body, straight to my pulsing pussy. The sensory overload has me close to reaching my climax.

"Look at me, Tink."

I straighten my head and open my eyes, giving Hook all of my attention. My heart stutters in my chest from the way he's looking at me. Like I'm his guiding North Star in the darkness that's slowly sweeping around us. Like he might actually love me.

The question is on the tip of my tongue. "Hook...."

If I ask him now, he has to tell me the truth. But I'm too fucking scared to ask. Too fucking scared of what the answer might be. Instead, I focus on my body and the orgasm that's about to flood through me.

"You're going to make me cum," I whisper.

"Don't close your eyes," he demands as he continues to fuck me in a steady rhythm. "Just look at me. Hold on to me."

And God, I do. I cling to him as my body shudders and spasms in his arms. We're bound together so tightly, physically and emotionally, that I don't know where my pleasure ends and his begins. His cock hardens even more, and I know he's about to cum, too. My eyes flutter but I force them open, locking them on Hook and the intense emotions I see reflected back at me in his.

"Fuck," he grunts as he thrusts into me, his rhythm finally lost to the pleasure. His forehead presses to mine. "Don't let go, Tink. Don't ever let go," he whispers against my lips as the euphoria swells around us.

Once we're back on the sandy beach, he helps dry me off by beating his wings like a fan around me. Then, he places his large shirt around my body before picking me back up and launching into the sky. I don't feel the cold as we fly back to the ship. His shirt is protecting my skin, and his body heat is sinking into me where I'm pressed against his chest.

I stare up into his handsome face as we fly, never taking my eyes off him. I'm sure the night sky is beautiful, and the water must look incredible with the light of the moon highlighting it, but I don't think anything can compare to the sight of Hook. If this was a cartoon, I'd be the character with big heart-eyes giving myself away, and I can't bring myself to care.

I know I'm safe in Hook's arms. I know he'd never let me fall physically, but he's the reason I'm falling anyway. The only question is, is he falling too? Even though I didn't ask it in the lagoon, I think I already know the answer. But I'm glad I didn't ask the question when he had no choice but to reply honestly. If he ever chooses to say those three little words to me, I want it to be his choice and his timing.

And all we have is time.

Chapter 20

The Summoning by Sleep Token

Taking her to the lagoon was both terrifying and exhilarating. I was worried she'd ask me how I felt, which honestly, I don't know if I'm ready to face yet. I know the truth deep down in my gut, and it would have come out in the truth waters of the lagoon, but in my mind, I'm still hesitant. I still don't know what the future holds and what that future will bear on us. But at least my concerns have been squashed.

Tink doesn't have feelings for Killian or Peter.

I feel like both of our hands were played, cards laid out for each other to see, but neither one of us wanted to look. They say actions speak louder than words, which in some cases is true, but in others, it's easy to assume they mean something they don't. There's just something special about hearing the words, hearing the verbal confessions of the heart, that seems to really prove a point.

Maybe that time will come for us, but I'm not going to worry about it right now. I'm just going to continue doing what we've been doing for the past few weeks, which is enjoying each other without expectations.

The entire crew is on deck, ready to welcome the new souls as Smee leads them on board. Two men and two women this time, all from dock H2. Smee should be happy with this turnout. Souls headed to Hell are always a rowdy bunch during the final days free of their Afterlife.

Standing at the top of the gangway, I shake each of their hands and welcome them onto the ship like I always do. As I greet the last woman, Tinkerbell's voice steals my focus.

"Jordan?"

Turning around, I find her staring at one of the men, a look of utter disbelief on her face. She looks like she's seen a ghost. My eyes dart to him. He looks just as shocked to see her but it's a different kind of shock. He looks almost...*guilty*.

"Tina," his voice shakes. "What are you doing here? I mean, how are you here?"

Tina? Was that her name when she was alive? My eyes keep darting back and forth between them, anxious to see what plays out. I don't know what's happening, but my gut tells me it's nothing good.

"I...I don't know." She shakes her head. Her eyebrows are pulled together tightly and it's clear she's grasping for memories. "I don't remember what happened to me, but I...I remember you."

Relief floods his face, and he rushes over to her, grabbing her face in his hands and kissing her. She stands just as frozen as I do, eyes wide and body tense.

When he breaks the kiss, he hugs her close to him. "Oh, Tina, I've missed you so much."

The crew all stop and stare at the exchange with dumbfounded looks on their faces. Red's small hands cover her mouth and Smee looks close to murder, no doubt on my behalf. Then, all eyes are on me. I mask my emotions, locking them down as tight as I can, but I still can't bring myself to move.

"We have so much to catch up on. Can we go somewhere and talk?" he asks eagerly.

Tink's eyes finally glance my way, but I can't read the look. Surely, after everything we've shared these past weeks, she's not going to allow this person to just show up out of the blue and end it all. Is she?

She looks away from me and finally nods. "Yeah, sure," she

agrees.

He takes her hand and leads her away from the crowd that's currently transfixed on the entire situation. He acts like he doesn't even notice he has an audience. Still too stunned to move, I watch them leave.

My insides are a fucking tsunami. Too many emotions swirl around inside me to acknowledge them all, but at the forefront is confusion. Coming in closely behind that is anger. Then there's possessiveness, jealousy, and the most painful one of all, coming in to crash against my ribcage, is loss. I can practically feel my heart splintering into pieces in my chest.

Did I just lose Tink?

Chapter 21

Demons by Written By Wolves

The second I saw his face, images of a past life flashed across my mind. A recording studio and stages, an apartment in a busy city, his face above mine as we made love.

It was like a dam being broken and I was in the direct path of the flood. It felt like I was drowning in a past that was a million miles away and also right in front of my face. The memories were so tangible, it felt like I could reach out and touch them.

And then, he kissed me.

I was too stunned to move. I was too stunned to process anything other than the life that was surging in my mind. A life I thought I'd lost. A life I had been ready to leave behind, but now, seeing it again…I'm not so sure.

If Hook felt anything at seeing Jordan kiss me, he didn't show it. Seeing that cold mask of indifference on his face hurt more than I'd like to admit. After the lagoon, I thought we'd crossed a line together. I was happy to go along for the ride and not question him further, not make him say what he was feeling or what he expected, and now, I guess I'm glad I didn't. I don't think it would have been what I wanted to hear.

Because he watched another man pull me away from him and he didn't so much as raise a finger to stop it. He didn't reach for me. He didn't claim me.

"Tina, are you ok?"

Jordan's voice pulls me out of my thoughts. I'm met with concerned, rich brown eyes inspecting me. Eyes I've stared into a hundred times before. I take in the rest of him; thick brown hair styled to perfection, a round face but not soft, and lips that leave a bit to be desired. He's perfectly handsome in a Hollywood kind of way, but since being here, surrounded by Hook and Sinn, hell, even Smee, he's utterly average. But I know deep down in my gut, I was head over heels in love with him.

His hand is on my cheek, and I grab his wrist, pulling it away as I put distance between us. I stand up from where I had been sitting on my bed and begin to pace.

"I'm ok. I'm just…really confused. I haven't had memories of my life before, until now. Until I saw you." I stop to face him. "Do you know what happened to me? Do you know how I died?"

He stares at me for a few seconds, quietly contemplating my question. He looks at me almost suspiciously, as if I'm trying to trick him.

"You really don't remember?"

I let out an exasperated breath and throw my hands up. "For fuck's sake, Jordan, why would I lie about that?"

"Ok, ok!" He stands and walks over to me, pulling my hands into his. "Tell me what you do remember."

Closing my eyes, I take a deep breath and reach for the memories. "My name is Tina LaBelle, and I was a pop singer. I…I remember being signed to a label and a big announcement party." I squeeze my eyes shut, trying to rifle through the chaotic memories. "I remember announcing a tour and then…nothing." I release a heavy sigh and open my eyes, pleading for him to give me the answers I'm so desperately seeking.

"Yes. All of that is true. I was your manager and also your fiancé, and Natalie was one of your backup singers and your *best* friend. We hardly did anything without each other. The three of us were inseparable. Do you remember her?"

Closing my eyes again, I see flashes of a blonde girl smiling at me, but then flashes of that same blonde girl kissing Jordan when they thought I wasn't around.

"Kind of," I lie. "The memories are fuzzy."

"That's ok." He reaches for my cheek again. "They'll come back. And even if they don't, I'm here now."

Grabbing his wrist again, I step back. "Jordan, you didn't answer my question. What happened to me? And how did *you* get here?"

"There was an accident during one of your camera block rehearsals. You were supposed to make an entrance from above the stage, but something happened with the harness, and you fell."

Flashes of Jordan and Natalie up on a scaffolding with me come and go but I can't grab ahold of a solid memory. Probably because it led to my death and I'm blocking it out.

"Was I…in pain?"

He shakes his head and swallows. "I don't think so."

But there's something in his eyes that tells me he's lying. Something in my gut is screaming at me not to trust him but I don't know why. Since I have no concrete evidence, I push those feelings aside.

I nod. "Okay. And what about you?"

He hangs his head, not wanting to meet my gaze. "Accidental overdose."

"What?!" I gasp. "We never did drugs. We always agreed that we'd stay away from that kind of life. What happened?"

He shrugs. "Things changed after…the accident."

"Oh my God."

I sit back on the bed and rest my head in my hands. This is all too much to handle. I feel entirely overwhelmed and conflicted. Now that I have memories coming back, I also have feelings coming back. Feelings for Jordan. Someone I spent most of my life with. He and Natalie had been with me from the beginning. Not just the beginning of my career, but since high school. They were so much more than just friends and a lover; they were my only family.

But then a memory of them kissing comes back. I remember confronting them and the hot tears of betrayal burning my cheeks as they both tried to deny it and play it off.

Then, there's my life now. My feelings for Hook. The new family I've come to find in the crew. It's all thrown together and fighting for dominance. The familiar burn of hot tears traces down my cheeks and I choke on the sobs that I'm trying to keep down.

"Tina." Jordan kneels before me, trying to get my attention.

"No." I shake my head. "My name is Tinkerbell. I haven't been Tina for a very long time."

He opens his mouth to say something but I stop him.

"I need to be alone."

"But I—"

"Leave." I glare at him, giving him one of the famous cold and angry Tinkerbell stares I'm so known for.

He nods and stands. "I'll give you some time to think about everything."

When the door clicks shut behind him, I run to it and lock it, then slide down to sit on the floor, pulling my knees into my chest. The pang of familiarity shoots through my chest. It feels like I'm back to day one on this ship, utterly alone.

Chapter 22

Heart In Your Hands by Wearing Scars

After Tink walked away, the crew tried to console me, but I wanted no part of it. I yelled at them to get the fuck away from me. I never yell. I think that was enough to let them know that no, I'm not ok, but to leave me the hell alone.

I've been standing at the prow since we left port, staring out into the darkness of the ocean, feeling for the first time since becoming the captain of this ship like I'm unsteady on my feet. Like I can't navigate my way through the darkness. Like the darkness will devour this ship and send us crashing against a rock or cliff.

I wanted to stop her from leaving but what right did I have to do that? What right do I have to stop her from learning about her life? The one she's been trying to remember and could finally get answers to. In the moment, it was her choice to make, and she made it.

I'm so lost in my raging thoughts that I don't hear her approach until she's standing right behind me.

"Hook."

Hearing her voice makes me flinch. I can't stop seeing him kiss her. I'm so pissed off, the last thing I want to do right now is talk to her.

"Hook, please talk to me."

The emotion in her voice breaks me. When I turn around and see tears shining in her eyes, everything else washes away. All that matters is her.

I'm on her in a second. How I manage to gently cup her face in my hands when all I feel is rage is proof of how much she means to me.

"What is it? Is it that motherfucker from your past? Did he hurt you? I swear to God, if he hurt you, I will fucking end him," I say through clenched teeth.

She tries to smile but fails. "Don't be ridiculous. You're not Sinn, Hook. You're not a killer."

"For you, I will be. Make no mistake about that, Tink. I will damn myself to this realm for eternity if it means protecting you."

The truth of my words shocks me more than anything else that's happened tonight. I would give up Heaven for her if meant keeping her safe. Keeping her in my arms. It's impossible to ignore what that means. I love her. I think I've been falling in love with her every day since talking to her on the rail that first day on the ship. She was trying so hard to be strong and brave, but I saw underneath her mask. And when I wanted to strangle my brother for leaving those bruises on her neck, I should have known I'd always want to protect her.

"He didn't do anything. At least, not here." She looks up at me with so much confusion and fear in her eyes, it startles me. "But I think he hurt me when I was alive. I think...I think he hurt me bad, Hook."

"Are you remembering?" I ask softly.

She opens her mouth to speak but no words come out. My hands no longer hold her face but sink into air. Right before my eyes, Tinkerbell starts to fade away.

"Tink, what's happening?" My voice is panicked as I try to grab on to her but it's no use. She's like a hologram image of herself, slowly disappearing. I see the same panic in her eyes as she reaches for me, her mouth screaming my name, but I can't hear it. I can't hear her, and I can't touch her.

"Tinkerbell!" I yell, desperately trying to bring her back.

I'm left standing alone on the deck, my hands grasping at

nothing but air. Only her lingering scent is proof that she was ever here at all, but it's gone just as quickly on the breeze.

She's gone.

I blink. What the fuck just happened. She's fucking gone. Did she cross over? But that's impossible. You can't just magically cross over into your Afterlife. You have to physically walk through The Gates. Did she…I swallow down my rising hysteria. Did she die?

Something inside of me snaps and I run. I land below deck like a hurricane crashing onto land.

"Where are you, you motherfucker?!" I yell for him.

Barreling into the lounge, I find him with the rest of the crew and souls. I grab him by the collar of his shirt and lift his sorry ass off the ground, yelling into his piece of shit face.

"What did you do to her?!"

"What the hell, man? I didn't do anything."

"Hook! Put him down." Smee slides up next to me, placing a hand on my shoulder, trying to get my attention.

"Don't lie to me!"

"Hook, what happened? Where's Tink?" Sasha asks in a calm voice. She always sees what the others miss.

"She's gone!" My voice cracks as I struggle to maintain control and not break.

"What do you mean she's gone?" Red joins in.

"Gone!" I yell again. "She literally just fucking disappeared! And this motherfucker did it!"

"I didn't do anything! Not here, at least. I—"

"What. Did. You. Do?" I grit my teeth, snarling in his face.

"She was always so weak. Such a fucking pushover. I didn't mean to hurt her, but she was in my way."

That's all I allow him to say. I set him down on his feet, keeping one hand fisted in his shirt, the other punching through his chest. I can feel his soul swirling around, alive in his chest. I grip it in my fist and yank it out.

His soul is not something the others can physically see, not like I can, but they all see the life drain out of his eyes. I let him go and he crumples to the floor at my feet. I stagger backwards and then I'm on my knees.

My wings are gone.

Tinkerbell is gone.

My life is gone.

Chapter 23

Calling by Fame On Fire

Beep.

    Beep.

        Beep.

The familiar sound pulls me from the deepest, darkest sleep I've ever had. But instead of the sound fading away as I wake like it usually does, it gets louder.

I blink into a bright, white room. The sound of the beeping is coming from a machine next to my bed. A quick sweep of the room tells me exactly where I am.

A hospital.

Immediately, I start to panic. I'm about to scream for help when a familiar voice stops me.

"Hello, Tink."

My eyes shoot to the door where the Angel of Death is leaning casually against the doorframe.

"Sinn?" My voice is scratchy and feels weak, making me cough. I push myself into a sitting position, trying to orient myself with everything that's happening.

He pushes off the doorframe and walks into my room. I watch as he pours a glass of water and hands it to me before sitting in the chair next to my bed.

The water feels refreshing as it slides down my throat, easing the tingle. "Thank you," I finally manage to say.

I stare into my empty cup for a long time, unsure of what to say or even what to think. Just a moment ago, I was standing on the Jolly Roger in front of Hook and then everything went black, and I woke up here. My brain is foggy, and I can't seem to clear it.

"What happened?" I finally ask, looking up at the angel I spent a hundred and fifty years pining for, only to be disappointed that he's not the angel I want to see. "Does this mean I'm dead?"

He shakes his head. "You're not dead, Tink. You're very much alive."

"I…I don't understand. I was in Purgatory for…for a really long time. How can I be alive?"

"Purgatory is also Limbo. You were in a state between life and death the entire time you were there. I think that's why it was harder for you to remember your life, because you had one foot in each world."

"How?"

"You still don't remember?" he questions, raising an eyebrow suspiciously.

Closing my eyes, I open my mind up to all the memories clawing to get through. Jordan and Natalie kissing was real. Me confronting them was real. And when I climbed up the ladder to the scaffolding way above the stage, prepared to get in my harness and rehearse, they were waiting for me.

They trapped me between them with no way to escape. They admitted they'd been seeing each other for years behind my back. Natalie was tired of being in my shadow and Jordan admitted he never loved me. He was only with me for the fame but that was going to change. They had plans to put Natalie in the spotlight. All they had to do was get me out of the picture.

"They tried to kill me," I whisper.

Sinn nods. "You've been in a coma for three years. Well, three years on Earth."

"That's why I never felt a pull to my Afterlife. Because I wasn't dead."

"Yes."

I lean back into the pillows and push my palms into my eyes, trying to stop the flood of memories. It's like a USB drive has been plugged in and I'm downloading my entire life in seconds. And the last memories to process are from the last few weeks.

"Hook," I mumble as tears push against my eyelids. I swear, I literally feel my heart crack.

"Aren't you going to ask why I'm here?" Sinn's cold voice reminds me that he's still here.

Wiping at my eyes, I take in a shaky breath and meet his gaze. "Are you here to punish me for what I did to Wendee?"

His jaw ticks, no doubt the mention of what happened replaying in his mind. I can almost feel his angry hands wrapping around my throat all over again.

"As much as that might please me, I'm not going to lose the only other person who's ever cared about me by being selfish."

Once again, I shake my head. "I don't understand."

"I'm here for Hook, Tinkerbell. Not for you," he growls out. "I love my brother. And, as much as it irks me, he seems to love you."

I swallow. Hearing those words from Sinn makes my heart race and hope bloom in my chest.

"If you don't love him back then tell me now and we'll be done here. It won't be easy delivering the news, but I will, and he'll move on."

"And if I do...love him?"

"You can't be with him if you're alive. Obviously."

"I have to die."

He nods. "And I can't do it for you."

His words take a few seconds to register, but once they do,

I'm not sure I really have a choice.

"But, if I...," I hesitate saying the words, "*kill* myself...I'll go to Hell. Hook is an angel. If I'm going to spend eternity with him, don't I need to go to Heaven?"

He lets out a frustrated breath, running a hand through his hair. "Hook lost his wings." He looks truly pained as he says it, and I feel the same pain pierce my chest. Hook's beautiful wings. Gone. He loved to fly.

I have to swallow down the thick ball of emotion clogging my throat before I can ask, "How?"

"When you disappeared, he took it out on your ex. Ripped his soul from his body. As angels, we're not supposed to interfere with lives in that way. It's what lost me my wings, too."

A sob escapes my throat as I think of Hook damning himself for me. I hate that he did it. I hate all of this. It's not fair. None of this has been fair. But what's done is done. This is our reality. And if there's one thing I know with everything that I am, it's that I want to be with Hook.

"What do I do?" I ask, lifting my chin with determination.

He nods to the side table next to me where a bottle and syringe magically appear. "Pump that into your IV and you'll fall asleep peacefully. You won't feel any pain."

My question from earlier remains unanswered, so I ask again. "Won't I go to Hell?"

"That's why I'm here." He smirks, the arrogant bastard. "To escort you to Purgatory instead."

I nod and purse my lips together, staring at the bottle and syringe. Thinking back on my life here on Earth, everything that I now remember, compared to the last few weeks I spent on the ship with Hook and the crew, it's not even a question.

Reaching for the bottle and syringe, I pull in as much of

whatever is in the bottle as I can, grab the IV, and inject it without a single moment of hesitation.

I catch Sinn's gaze as I remove the syringe and I think I see the smallest glimmer of something warm pass through his cold blue eyes. Before I can look harder, or ask any more questions, I feel darkness pulling me under. My entire body relaxes. It feels like my bones melt. I lie back, closing my eyes but I don't see Sinn's eyes.

I see the clearest, brightest, turquoise waters below me. I spread out my arms, a smile on my face and the wind in my hair as I fall.

Fall.

Fall.

Fall.

Chapter 24

Half Life by Livingston

As soon as I was able to control my emotions and pick myself up off the floor, I immediately turned the Jolly Roger around and went back to port. If there was anyone that was going to have answers for me, it was my brother.

Afterall, he knows every soul's story.

He was hesitant to tell me anything. It's not his place to divulge a soul's story, but seeing my broken desperation, I think he took pity on me. Or maybe it was Wendee's urging that got him to agree. Either way, we came up with a plan, and that plan was contingent on one factor.

Whether or not Tink loves me.

As I wait impatiently at the lagoon, I can't help the doubt creeping in with every second that ticks by. Standing at the edge of the water, eyes scanning the surface frantically, I wait with my heart pounding and blood rushing in my ears.

A shadow down below catches my attention, followed by bubbles that breach the surface. I wait with bated breath, hands wringing together with my nervous energy.

Then, she bursts through the surface. A spot of bright green amongst the light blue. She gasps for air, and it feels like she's being reborn. Like this is the start of her new life. The start of *our* new life.

I charge into the water like a madman. As soon as Tink sees me, she's scrambling through the water trying to reach me, too. We slam together, arms wrapping around each other and lips crashing.

It's messy and chaotic and filled with so much fucking emotion.

I grab her face and whisper in between kisses, "You're here. You're really here." I kiss her again. "I thought I lost you."

"I'm here," she says breathlessly. "You can't get rid of me that easy."

I rest my forehead on hers and take a deep breath. For the first time since she disappeared, the pain in my chest is gone. "Do you remember when we first kissed, you bit my lip and thought you'd hurt me?"

She giggles. "Yes."

"And I said that you could never hurt me." I pull back to look at her. "It was a lie. I've never felt pain like I felt when you disappeared right through my hands."

"Hook...." Her voice is soft, and her eyes are so full of sympathy. "I didn't want to leave you."

"I know."

I take her mouth again, sliding my tongue against hers, trying to memorize how she tastes. How she feels in my arms. I will never take this, *her*, for granted ever again. She smiles against my lips, and I can't help but smile back. We kiss and laugh and stare at each other and then kiss some more. She finally draws back to look at me, a serious look overtaking her face.

"When I first joined your crew, I was so angry. But underneath that, I was lost. I was alone. I wished for death. I wished Sinn had taken my soul or fed me to Serene." She shakes her head. "I just couldn't imagine a future. I didn't see the point of living. Until you. I was asleep for a hundred and fifty years, but you woke me up, Hook."

"I love you."

"I love you."

We both say it at the same time.

She laughs joyfully, but I cup her face in my hands and hold on to her stare like it's my lifeline. I need her to know how much she's changed me, too.

"I've never seen a future here either. I never truly committed to this life. I've been surrounded by such amazing people, but I never let anyone in. I kept everyone at arms-length but then here you come, a feisty little viper that sank her fangs into me and didn't let go. You broke down my barriers like they were nothing. You ripped open my chest and exposed my heart, showing me pieces I've never seen before. I'm a better man because of you, Tink."

She swallows down her emotion, tears running down her cheeks. I don't know if they're happy tears or not. "I'm sorry about your wings."

Shaking my head, I insist, "Please, don't be. I knew the consequences of my actions and it was a price I was willing to pay. I knew the moment you disappeared that I would do anything to get you back. I knew my place was never again going to be in Heaven. My place is here, with you."

I kiss her tear-streaked cheeks and then softly lay my lips on hers. I kiss her slowly. Deeply. And now that everything else has been said, my body responds to the kiss. My dick hardens and I rub it across her pussy, drawing a beautiful moan from her throat.

"Can I make love to you, Tink?"

"Yes," she says eagerly. "Make love to me, Hook."

I pull back to look into her sparkling hazel eyes as I push inside her. Then she destroys me with a devastating smile, full of all the love I feel inside me.

This is Heaven.

I'm home.

Epilogue – 1 year later

"Oh, come one!" Smee pleads. "It's not *that* bad."

Glancing around the kitchen island, I see everyone grimacing and spitting out their mouthful of food into napkins, just like I am. Except Red, who just sticks her tongue out and lets the meatloaf fall right onto her plate with a look of pure disgust on her face.

"That can't even be considered food," she says as she wipes her tongue with her napkin before taking a huge chug of wine. When she gargles it in a dramatic display, I can't help but laugh out loud.

"Oh, not you too, princess. Seriously?" He looks around and everyone is laughing and shaking their heads.

"I didn't even know it was possible to fuck something up this badly," Killian chimes in.

"Let's agree to not ever let Smee attempt to cook for us again," Fin says with a curl to his lip.

"Are you guys just fucking with me?" Smee takes a bite of the meatloaf, talking around it. "It's not that bad. I don't know what you guys are talking about."

"Well then, there's plenty for you." Sasha pushes her plate away from her.

"I'll put pizza in the oven," Hook suggests, patting me on the ass so I'll let him out of the barstool.

"Good idea." I kiss him as he slides out from under me.

"You just need to stay in your lane, dude," Red says. "Stick to what you're good at."

"You mean like flirting and fucking." He smirks and wiggles his eyebrows.

I snort and Sasha rolls her eyes, but she smiles. Red laughs out loud and Killian just shakes his head.

"Don't act like you guys don't love to watch the show," Smee pushes back. He climbs to his feet and a second later his shirt is off and flying toward my face.

I snag it and laugh as I throw it back at him, but he's oblivious as he throws himself to the floor and starts doing pushups. Red jumps up and throws herself onto his back like a monkey. To his credit, he still manages to do pushups easily, even with her weight on his back. Her giggles and Smee's smartass remarks make me smile.

This is my life now.

Surrounded by a group of people with so many different personalities, so many shenanigans, so many laughs, and so much sex…Jesus, the sex these people have. The sex *I'm* having. I sit back in the barstool and take a few moments to appreciate the moment. We're all sinners and far from perfect, but I've never felt more at home.

Hook's strong arms wrap around my chest from behind me. His sexy voice whispering in my ear makes me forget anyone else is around us. He utterly captivates all of my attention, every time he's near me.

"You need to eat dinner, but after that, prepare to be my dessert."

The promise of what's to come, knowing that devious mouth is going to be on my body soon, has me shivering. Just the thought has my pussy wet. I'm about to put up one hell of an argument and insist I don't need food, when Red suddenly appears beside me, grabbing my hand and yanking me out of Hook's hold.

"Let's sing karaoke until the pizza is ready!"

Laughing again, I let her pull me out of the kitchen, looking back to see Hook staring at me with a mixture of love and desire in his eyes.

"Are you coming?" I ask.

"Are you kidding? I wouldn't miss you singing for the world."

Biting my lip, I fight against the tears as my heart swells. I'll never get to live my dream of being a famous singer, but I'm more than happy to sing for my family, here on this ship.

And my biggest fan watching me sing like it's the first time he's heard me, every time.

Henry Hook.

My happily ever after.

Author's Note & Acknowledgements

As always, I'm incredible humbled and grateful when I get to this point in a manuscript. Three and a half years later, I still can't believe I'm an author. And an author that has a handful of loyal readers at that! To say it's an incredible feeling doesn't even come close to explaining how I feel. Just know that I am forever grateful for any and all support! I wouldn't be doing this without you.

I always have to shout my amazing artist, Cagla. You always bring my characters and ideas to life with the smallest input from me. You're so incredibly talented and such a lovely person. I look forward to our next project! And the next! And the next!

My Beta reader, Kara, who shines and polishes my messy words. My books would absolutely not be as high quality without you. I am so forever grateful for our partnership.

My social media family and ARC Team. You guys are seriously the BEST! I know I haven't been as social or as "present" as I have been in the past. Just know that I adore each and every one of you and so grateful to have you in my corner, hyping up every book!

For those of you who requested this story, I hope that I delivered and you loved Hook and Tink's story as much as I enjoyed writing it. And to anyone who has picked up and read one of my books. Thank you. From the bottom of my heart.

XOXO
Harmony

More From The Author

If you enjoyed this read, please check out my other books!

My Disney Reimaginings/Retellings.
Unforgivable Sins (light-dark Peter Pan)
Beastly Lies & Beautiful Legends (Sweet/Cozy Beauty & the Beast)
zero To HERO (light-dark Hercules)

Also, check out my complete urban/paranormal fantasy series, The Amarah Rey, Fey Warrior Series.
Awaken
Fey Blood
Dark Temptations
Divine Destiny

You can find them on Amazon here: Amazon Author page or the kindle version here: Amazon Ebooks/Kindle

Stay up to date on news and exclusive content and follow me on social media!

Instagram
TikTok
Newsletter

Thank you for being here and all of your support! Again, I could not do this without You. Leave those reviews 😊